WEIRDLY WALTER

JULIA WALTON

HARPER
An Imprint of HarperCollinsPublishers

Weirdly Walter

Copyright © 2024 by Julia Walton

All rights reserved. Printed in the United States of America. No part of this book may be used or reproduced in any manner whatsoever without written permission except in the case of brief quotations embodied in critical articles and reviews. For information address HarperCollins Children's Books, a division of HarperCollins Publishers, 195 Broadway, New York, NY 10007.

www.harpercollinschildrens.com

Library of Congress Control Number: 2023948478

ISBN 978-0-06-332496-1

Typography by Corina Lupp
24 25 26 27 28 LBC 5 4 3 2 1

FIRST EDITION

For Alex, Charlie, and Jamie
—J.W.

ONE

All great moments start with a choice.

THIS IS A PRETTY good quote from my dad, which is why I wrote it down in my orange journal.

But not everything Dad says is magical.

For example, I also wrote this one down:

Eat more fruit. If you can't poop, eat a pear. There's no excuse for constipation, Walter.

See what I mean?

But I think about that first one a lot.

All great moments start with a choice.

'Cuz he's right.

For me, it all started with the morning announcements.

I was waiting in the principal's office because that's what you do on your first day. You wait around so the principal can walk you to class and do that thing where they point at you in front of everyone and say:

This is the new kid. Everyone be nice to him.

Or something like that.

Only no one really cares. Everyone already has their friends.

And new kids are always different and weird.

I should know. I've been a new kid a lot. Three times this past year already.

One nice thing about being a new kid is that no one knows anything about you. No one knows about the time I barfed on the class hamster and my teacher had to give him a tiny, gross hamster bath in the sink. And no one knows that in third grade I wore dirty socks every single day for a whole month because we moved a lot and my dad kept forgetting to buy more.

Or do laundry.

So I was waiting in the office while a secretary with red fluffy hair kept looking at her watch. I got distracted by the way her shiny cat pin caught the light.

"He's late and I'm getting tired of covering for these kids. This is the third week in a row. He was supposed to be here ten minutes ago," she said to another really old lady sitting next to her. Cat Pin Lady looked a little bit like a raisin. Only I'd never say that to her because no one would want to be told they look like dried fruit.

Dad always says don't let stuff like that come spilling out of your mouth.

Actually, what I wrote down in the journal is:

> Once words slip out, there's no calling them back. Even if you apologize. They'll be printed in someone else's head forever. It's okay to use words to defend yourself, but they can hurt, so be careful with them.

I should probably mention Dad doesn't always follow his own advice. Once around Mother's Day last year, a teacher said, "I noticed you're not making a card with the rest of the class. Do you not have a mother?"

Which made me sad.

When my dad found out, he went to school and asked my teacher if she had a brain.

He said a few bad words too. I could hear him through the door.

It didn't matter. We were gone the following week anyway. Dad got another gig, and we were out.

For the record, I *do* have a mom. Everyone does. But I never knew my mom, and the truth is you can't miss someone you never knew. She left, and that was that.

Plus I never really needed to miss her because I have Dad.

Well, I did.

So, I finally got a look at raisin-face lady's name plate. Her name is Anita Butte.

There's no way kids don't call her Mrs. Butt.

Anyway . . . she leaned back and said, "Maryann, I'll have to read the announcements myself. If it gets too late, the teachers are going to have kittens about interrupting their class."

Old people say weird stuff.

Why do they say they'll have kittens when they mean that someone will get upset?

Why would having kittens make someone upset? People like kittens.

I mean, not me. Cats are pretty stupid, actually.

Except for Tiberius, the cat at my grandpa's house who sleeps on my bed now.

He's super old, but he's cool.

He follows me around and swishes his tail when I come home. He's like a dog, actually. But if the only reason I like him is because he acts like a dog, then I think it's still okay to say most cats are monsters, especially the ones who pee on your stuff when they're mad you left for the day.

My dad says when he was growing up, they had a cat named Squishy who would do this all the time. There's even a quote about him in the journal.

> Peeing on other people's stuff when they abandon you is a fairly effective way to demonstrate your feelings. Squishy knew <u>exactly</u> what he was doing.

Mrs. Butte stood up and took a deep breath like she was about to make a big speech on TV. She took a sheet of paper off the printer and laid it next to her glasses.

"Alright, Maryann. I'm going to get some water, and then I'm going to read the announcements."

Then someone poked their head into the office

and told them both to get a donut from the teacher's lounge before all the good ones were gone, and suddenly the front desk was deserted.

There was a small microphone on the desk with a blue button. It felt like I could make it jump into my hand if I thought about it hard enough.

Sometimes I like to pretend I can do stuff like that.

With the front desk being empty, I got up and walked over. The paper that Mrs. Butte had left behind was sitting there with a list of all the announcements for the week.

I was going to sit back down. Really, I promise I was. But there was something about that blue button.

I had to push it. I just had to.

So I did.

And then when I did, this voice just came out of me.

Someone else. Someone brave. Someone funny.

High-pitched and robotic.

Someone who, honestly, sounded a little bit like an alien.

Greetings, students of Apple Grove Performing Arts Academy.

I am Trox from the planet Pox.

These are the announcements for Monday, January fourteenth.

This week's lunch specials include processed meat in the form of hot dogs, hamburgers, meat loaf, and spaghetti.

Don't forget to bring your change for the bake sale on Wednesday.

Friday afternoon Mr. Thibodo will begin auditions for the spring play, **Willy Wonka and the Chocolate Factory.**

Have a productive day, humanoids.

Enjoy your lunchtime meat products of choice.

Trox signing off.

I clicked the blue button again, and I heard kids laughing all through the halls. Good laughing. The kind that happens when you say something funny. Not the kind that happens when you spill juice on your pants and it looks like you peed.

Then I turned around and there was the principal, Mrs. Pudumjee, looking at me with her arms crossed.

"This way, Walter," she said.

TWO

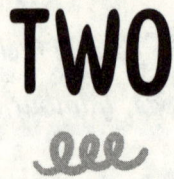

I DIDN'T EXPECT MRS. Pudumjee to be cool.

I mean cool for a principal.

Sometimes principals try to be your friend. Sometimes they tell you to come to them if you need to talk. They tell you that you can trust them and you don't have to worry.

But then sometimes you tell them something about your dad, and it changes everything.

They make a call, and hey, kid, you're at another new school.

Anyway, Mrs. Pudumjee was dressed kinda like a teacher who was wearing all the stuff out of the lost and found. Her bracelets said things like:

ACTION!

BE FEARLESS!

I AM AN APPLE GROVE PERFORMING ARTS ACADEMY SUPER SQUIRREL
TO THINE OWN SELF BE TRUE

But she was wearing makeup like a regular grown-up and her hair was pretty normal, except for the ends. It looked like someone had dipped the ends of her dark black hair in purple paint that you could only see when the light hit it just right. She was also wearing a school T-shirt that said "Apple Grove Performing Arts Academy," with a picture of a cartoon squirrel singing onstage.

When she sat down, she leaned back in her chair and then pointed to a seat in front of her desk. I expected her to yell at me or tell me that was no way to make a first impression or to do that thing where adults sigh like you've disappointed them.

But she didn't.

She made that face adults make when they know they probably *should* be mad at you for something but they're not. Like whenever I took out my dad's guitar, he'd pretend to be mad about it, but I know he secretly loved it.

Her office was filled with superhero posters.

Batman, Superman, Wonder Woman. But that wasn't the most impressive thing in the room. Behind her desk was a huge assortment of snacks. And it wasn't just the usual pretzels or a bag of gross cookies. There were tubes of mini M&M's. Bags of Swedish Fish. Pocky sticks. Habanero chili puffs. Dried shrimp. Top Ramen. Matcha green tea–flavored Kit Kats. And a bunch of other snack foods I'd never seen before in languages I couldn't read.

Plus an entire shelf of comic books.

"You have a favorite?" she asked.

"No, I don't read comics."

I wished I'd had a more interesting answer, but I'd actually never read a comic book before. That didn't seem to bother her.

She sat down in her chair and smiled.

"Can Trox come back next week?" she asked.

"Um. What?" I said.

"Trox. The alien voice you just did. That was his name, right?"

"Yeah," I said.

"Perfect," she said. "Our morning announcement person just quit—nerves, I think—so we need a replacement."

"You're not mad?" I asked.

She looked at me, and her mouth twisted into half a smile.

"Not yet," she said. "Next time you'll do it with permission, though."

She looked at her watch.

"Let's get you to class," she said standing up and leading me out of her office, toward a gate in the courtyard. She pushed it open and the first thing I saw was a massive tree covered in purple flowers. Like she'd opened a magical portal. The branches hung above the monkey bars, and when the light shone through it, it reminded me of a stained-glass window. That makes sense, since everything here is art. Even the trash cans have painted murals on them.

There's also a ton of open space covered in fake grass. I guess it's there just in case anyone needs to do a spontaneous cartwheel or flash mob.

Here in California, it seems like all the schools have hallways outside. Outside hallways are weird. It's like they don't think anyone is going to escape to the playground. That's a lot of trust.

But then, Apple Grove is an art school.

Dad had said that was part of the reason I was

staying with Grandpa, because Apple Grove Performing Arts Academy would be good for me.

He said, "Regular school tries to turn kids into robots. Not art school. Art school makes you weird on purpose."

He always talks like that. There is something like that in the orange journal too.

> *Don't be like everyone else, Walter.*
> *Be weird. Be kind.*
> *Find the music in life.*

That's not one of my favorite Dad quotes. It sounds like something someone's mom would have printed on a T-shirt in pretty, loopy writing.

Apple Grove wasn't around when my dad was a kid, but I guess that didn't matter because he became a musician anyway.

"How'd you get so good at doing voices?" Mrs. Pudumjee asked.

"It's just something I do with my dad," I said.

She smiled and said, "He really should have won, you know."

I smiled back.

He *is* a bit of a local legend, actually.

He was on this show called *Hometown Tunes* when I was little. It was a competition against people from small towns all over the country, and he *almost* won. Lots of people called in to vote for him, so it was kinda shocking when he lost to a girl from Rhode Island who could sing opera.

Anyway, he's a little bit famous from that. Still gets recognized sometimes, like once when we were out getting burgers. He even wrote a song that gets played on the radio sometimes. People recognize his name and go, "Oh yeah, that rocker guy from *Hometown Tunes*. I liked him."

I looked down at my feet, trying to keep up as Mrs. Pudumjee zipped across the school. That's when I noticed that my feet were covered in rainbow chalk dust.

"Oh, those are our Chalk Walk entries," said Mrs. Pudumjee, following my gaze and pointing to the murals all over the ground. "Pretty great, right? Students work on those in teams and then we vote on our favorites."

There was a mural of a tiger that looked like it was going to jump out of the concrete and another one of three witches stirring a cauldron. I wouldn't want to be the one to ruin them.

"You really just wash these off when the contest is over?"

That made me a little sad.

Mrs. Pudumjee smiled.

"We take lots of photos. Then we make room for new art!"

Her bracelets jingled like tiny bells as she waved her hand at the ground.

She stopped in front of a door with a number five on it.

"Ready for fifth grade?"

I nodded, but even if I wasn't ready, I don't think it would have changed anything.

"Good morning, Mrs. Pudumjee!"

Everyone sang it together like a choir. I guess that's a thing here to stand up whenever someone comes in because Mrs. Pudumjee laughed and put her hands up to get everyone to sit down.

"Hi, Mr. Lopez. Hi, class. This is Walter. He just did the morning announcements."

Some kids laughed, and one girl with a ponytail full of wavy brown hair raised her hand and said,

"You did the alien voice?"

I nodded, and she smiled.

"This is Walter's first day here. So everyone show him an Apple Grove Performing Arts Academy welcome, okay?"

Mrs. Pudumjee lowered her glasses with a pretend serious face, and just as she was about to leave, a boy in the middle of the room said, "Why's he here in January? Why didn't he start in September with everyone else?"

It wasn't a mean question. But anyone can make something sound mean if they use the right voice and make the right face.

It's actually a lot of effort to look mean.

And Mrs. Pudumjee looked like she was going to jump in and say something, but I just said, "Guess we start school in January on my planet."

A few people laughed, and the kid who asked the questions didn't smile.

"You can sit in that seat near Filomena," said Mr. Lopez.

The girl with the wavy brown hair and glasses waved at me, and I sat down.

"You can call me Fil," she whispered.

* * *

My grandpa picked me up from school in his old work truck. He still has it even though he's retired.

I don't think he's like a regular grandpa, because he doesn't have hard candies or a recliner. He also doesn't nap.

He goes to the gym every day to run on the treadmill and lift weights.

His garden has zero weeds because he pulls them every morning.

On Monday he goes grocery shopping.

On Thursday he washes his truck.

He only really believes in one thing.

Routine.

And I guess getting donuts every Sunday morning is also a regular grandpa thing. It's one of his routines I actually like.

"Look," he told me when I moved in. "You gotta keep busy. It's the only thing that keeps your head on straight. You have to keep your mind and body going all the time or else you wind up doing stuff you shouldn't be doing."

I know he said that because of Dad, but he doesn't mention him if he can help it. He just brings me the phone whenever Dad calls and then walks back out into the hall to let me talk to him alone.

Dad is the one who asks about my day and what I'm learning and what kinds of things I'm doing with Grandpa.

"You did an alien voice?" Dad asked when he called later. So I did it for him, and he laughed.

My dad's laugh is my favorite sound on the planet because it's real. He never does a fake laugh if something isn't funny.

"Did you meet anyone today?" he asked.

So I told him about Fil and that I sat next to her at lunch and that outdoor schools in California are weird and then I told him they were going to do a *Willy Wonka and the Chocolate Factory* play at school.

I could hear him smile over the phone. Which I know sounds weird, but you can just tell when someone smiles over the phone. There's this crinkly noise they make at the corner of their mouth like they're unwrapping a candy.

"I love that one," he said.

"I know, Dad. We've watched it a million times," I said. "When are you coming to get me?"

It had only been a few weeks, but I always asked when I thought it was getting close to the end of the phone call because Dad always stopped talking after I said it. And I wanted to hear him talk for as long as possible, but still I wanted to know if this time he was going to say, *I'll be back tomorrow.*

"Soon, I hope," he said. "I love you. Be good for Grandpa."

Then he hung up. So I put the phone down, and Tiberius jumped on my bed and curled up into a big fat orange fluff ball.

I heard my grandpa call upstairs that dinner was ready.

He always seems to know when the call is over.

When I went downstairs, Grandpa had set the table. He put two small purple gummy vitamins next to my water glass, and he folded a napkin under my fork.

He'd made a baked ziti with marinara sauce and lots of cheese.

I ate two bowls. Grandpa's mouth twitched up into a smile when I scooped the second one.

Dad usually let me have cereal or bagel bites for dinner, but this was good, too.

The only sucky part is that Grandpa says I have to eat vegetables.

The first night, he put a small bowl of broccoli in front of me. I told him, "I don't eat vegetables."

He said, "You do now."

I said, "But I don't like vegetables."

Then he looked at me and said, "In this house, you eat your greens."

And I said, "Dad never makes me eat stuff I don't like."

So Grandpa leaned forward in his chair and said, "You are not getting scurvy on my watch."

"What's scurvy?" I asked.

He made me look it up, and it's really gross.

Your gums bleed, and your teeth fall out. Then there are sores and pus.

I guess pirates got it a lot because they didn't get that many vegetables when they were at sea.

So now I eat my vegetables. Because I like my teeth where they are.

THREE

WHEN DAD EATS A hot dog, he loads it with stuff.

There's always ketchup and mustard. Usually relish. And sauerkraut and onions if they have them. But once in a while Dad would take me to a place that served fancy hot dogs. He'd always get something crazy—like one with bleu cheese, arugula, grilled onions, and crunchy ramen noodles. And that's when I found out grown-ups don't always make good choices.

Dad is not perfect, but he's still my favorite person.

Every morning when I brush my teeth, I picture him standing next to me because we used to brush our teeth at the same time every day. Together.

One bathroom, you know.

He said he always remembered to do it, because he had to make sure I was doing it too.

The mouthwash was the tricky part. He'd always pretend to spit it out at the same time as me to make me laugh. Sometimes we did, and it was gross.

I looked over to my mouthwash cup. The orange journal was sitting right there.

Sometimes I'll turn to a random page to see what thoughts I wrote down from Dad that day. It's like opening a fortune cookie. There's this weird magic that makes it seem like he's in the room with me.

Like the time I was feeling sad, and I opened the journal to the page where I wrote down something Dad said on a long car ride once when we were both feeling bummed about missing a train to Baltimore.

> *If you ever find yourself feeling sad for no apparent reason, I'd like you to remember that time we went to the hospital for your ear infection and that really ridiculously old guy walked down the hallway in front of us in his walker with his bare white butt hanging out of his gown. Remember what he said? Take a nice loooong look, ladies. These cheeks are antique! Then see how sad you feel. Laughing is not overrated.*

Most of the entries are completely useless because Dad is the sort of guy who says whatever is floating through his head the minute he thinks it. So in a way, even though the journal does not always solve problems or make sense, it always does the trick to remind me that he's still around somewhere.

This morning it would have been really cool if I could have just turned to one of the pages and gotten a quote from Dad about what it means to miss someone. Or what it means to be brave. But instead I got this:

Pie is better than cake, and oatmeal raisin cookies are garbage.

Thanks, Dad.

So I stuffed the journal into my backpack and put on a T-shirt and shorts.

We actually had to buy more shorts for California because the weather never changes here. I'm not used to wearing shorts in October.

When I got to school, I followed the crowd of kids walking through the gates. It's a pretty normal school for the most part, even if I did pass a group of kids juggling bean bags on their way in.

At Apple Grove everybody has a thing. The idea is that once you graduate from here, you go to Orchard Hills Performing Arts High School. This is like the training wheels for that. There aren't that many art schools for younger kids. Like, they usually want you to wait a little bit to be weird.

"So you got in for playing the guitar?" Fil asked when I met her outside our first class, which I think was PE, because everyone came out holding broken planks of wood. They must have been doing a section on karate.

"Yeah," I said. "It's my dad's guitar. He plays, and he taught me a few songs, so . . ."

"I guess they'll let anybody into this place," said Travis, the mean kid who asked why I started school in January, as he shoved past me in the hall.

"Your butt cream commercial sucked, Travis," said Fil. He smirked at us but didn't look like he'd even heard Fil.

"He thinks he's a real actor because he landed a commercial and some modeling work as a baby," Fil explained. She rolled her eyes as he tossed a half-eaten bagel in the trash can and followed some of the other kids to class.

"Well, at least it's not the ukulele," said Fil. "*Everybody* plays the ukulele here, and nobody plays it well. And if I hear a crappy version of 'Somewhere over the Rainbow' one more time . . ."

She made a face like she was going to throw up.

"And you're here for . . . ?" I asked.

"Dance," she said, twirling her wrists dramatically. "But only because they don't have gymnastics."

"So you wanna, like, be in the Olympics someday?"

"Nope. I wanna be a vet. I just like walking on my hands and doing flips."

Like I said, they have regular school stuff at Apple Grove too. It's not like they just let you finger paint and dance around all day, which is what my grandpa thought before he did the tour.

The cool thing is that even in the "real" classes, they let you do all sorts of fun extra stuff.

There's a science class you can take on plants where you work in the school vegetable gardens. Sometimes they let you do math outside with chalk. And Fil says that some older kids get to use the auditorium to act out major moments in history for their social studies classes.

All of this probably seems like a ton of information for only being here a couple days, but that's Apple Grove. They want you to feel free to express yourself.

I told Grandpa this, and he snorted. Not in the way that means he thinks something is stupid, but in the way that means he's thinking about it and it sounds like it might be okay.

I think it might be okay too.

But there's a good chance it would probably suck if Fil weren't here.

I was glad to see Fil again after yesterday. This whole being-friends-with-her situation happened pretty quick, but I guess it just made sense. From almost the moment we met, we started doing this thing where she starts saying a line from a movie or a cartoon that she doesn't think I'll know, and I finish it. And she laughs every time.

She has no idea how much TV I have watched.

Then she'll ask me about the voices I do and let me practice.

It's like a tiny routine that only took us zero time to figure out.

Grandpa would be proud.

"Do Kermit the Frog!" she'll say or, "Do Sponge-Bob!"

Every time I do an impression, I picture the actual character standing right next to me. Kermit. The Queen. Darth Vader.

But when I make up a voice . . . it's just me as that voice.

So, like, me if I were an alien. Me if I were a surfer. Or something weird, like a lobster or a giant pimple. And yeah, I know that's probably not something other people think about, but sometimes I just stare into my bathroom mirror and voices come out.

Dad used to be the one standing there laughing when I practiced. Now Fil tells me which ones are good and which ones suck, even though she doesn't actually say they suck. She's nice about it. She just says they "need work."

"But Mr. Thibodo can help you with that. He's the acting coach here."

She pointed to the open door in the hallway outside

where someone was hanging up bright orange flyers.

When I first saw him, Mr. Thibodo reminded me of my grandpa 'cuz he's an old guy who doesn't act old. He looked like he was about to perform something 'cuz even Mr. Thibodo's walk kinda looks like a dance. So that part is definitely not like Grandpa.

He also has thick glasses with silver frames and a gray (actually almost white) Afro.

"I want to be Veruca Salt," Fil said after Mr. Thibodo walked past the playground to high-five some second graders. "The really bratty one who whines for everything," she added.

I know who Veruca is.

I knew her entire song by heart because it was one of the only movies we had at our last apartment. My dad and I watched it all the time. Especially when he got one of his headaches and had to rest for a while.

He even had his own version of that song "Pure Imagination." He'd play the introduction even slower than the movie, so even if I was listening to someone else play the song at the bus stop or something, I would know if it was him without having to look up.

Fast. Slow. Fast. Fast. Slow.

"Who do you want to be?" Fil asked.

"Nobody."

She looked at me.

"You're great with voices. I bet they make you Charlie."

"Doubt it," said someone behind us. It was Travis, of course. He was giving me the same look he'd given me that first day in class. Like he was shooting meanness out of his eyes.

He wrote his name down on the audition sign-up sheet with the pencil someone had tied to the wall and then dropped it so it swung against the bulletin board with a smack.

Fil narrowed her eyes at him, and I laughed.

"What part would you want?" Fil asked, pretending Travis wasn't there.

"Maybe an Oompa Loompa," I said.

"You can do better than an Oompa Loompa," she said.

"How do you know?" I asked her.

"I just do," she said. "And I'm always right," she added. "Ask anyone. Except my sister."

Fil reminds me of something Dad used to say a lot. I wrote it inside the back cover of the journal.

The best people are the ones who can say nothing and everything at the same time.

I didn't really know what that meant before, but after school that first day, while we were waiting on the playground to get picked up, Fil gave me her last pink starburst and ate the yellow one.

Nobody likes yellow more than pink.

My grandpa arrived to pick me up from school at the same time as Fil's mom. She introduced herself enthusiastically, and my grandpa nodded at her. He's not always great with people.

"Got all your stuff?" Grandpa asked me.

He just said it so he'd have something to say, because he could already see that I was wearing my backpack, so I had to already have all my stuff. But I nodded anyway.

"See you tomorrow, Wally."

"Bye, Fil."

Grandpa raised an eyebrow.

She'd just started calling me Wally.

And it's a stupid name.

But if I'm being honest, Fil is a stupid name too. And it's kinda cool to get a nickname.

Unless that nickname is Tapioca Butt. Then it's probably time to move again.

When I got home, Tiberius looked at me like I'd just interrupted his busy schedule. Like he hadn't just spent seven hours with his furry butt on MY pillow.

But tonight, it's almost like he knows that I'm distracted, so he scoots off my bed and flicks his tail back and forth in my direction as he goes.

Some nights Dad doesn't call, and I just kinda flip through my journal and try not to let the silence bug me. When Dad is around, there is never silence. There's music. Or movement. Or something you can listen to.

Dad is also just a super noisy guy. Like in the early morning when he's trying to be quiet, he'll still open cabinets too hard and then say SHHHH to no one when they slam. At night he snores, and it sounds like when you blow one of those cheap plastic whistles they give in gift bags at birthday parties.

And when he takes a phone call, his voice is always louder than it actually needs to be.

Silence sucks when you're used to noise.

But I tried to ignore it by flipping through the orange journal.

Cracking your knuckles is one of the greatest feelings in the world. It's like releasing tiny slimy demons that live in your bones.

Dad cracks his knuckles all the time. It's funny how you can miss a gross-sounding noise.

Heaven is a chocolate éclair.

Dad likes a lot of different kinds of food. Especially sweet stuff. He'd grab a dropped cookie off the ground if he wanted it bad enough.

If you ever meet the Queen (STAY WITH ME, WALTER), make sure you eat before you go. A sandwich, a banana, a cracker—anything. Do not be that guy that lets their stomach erupt with that horrible gurgly noise so you're left wondering for the rest of your life if the Queen of England thought you farted.

He is *so* weird.

But then he's serious a lot too. Like this:

> It's not important to be nice.
>
> "Nice" is a weak word. Like a Christmas card that you throw away anyway.
>
> But it *is* important to be good.
>
> Good is different.
>
> And don't let people get you mixed up about good and bad. People will try to tell you that it's a fine line. That some people are misunderstood.
>
> But it's something you feel in your bones.
>
> It's that feeling you get when someone bad walks into a room, and all the juices in your belly try to crawl up your throat. Trust that.
>
> Because someone who is good might not be the easiest person to deal with, and someone who is very nice can still be the worst person you ever met.

Sometimes I just put my hand on the notebook. I don't know why.

Maybe I'm expecting something amazing to happen. Like he's trapped in the book because all his words are in there and if I just open the right page at the right time, maybe he'll jump out of it with his guitar.

Then I think about when I first started this journal.

I started writing down the stuff Dad said because it was funny and because I didn't want to forget. I hate forgetting something important and then spending all sorts of time trying to remember the thing I forgot. It sucks. And the stuff Dad says is usually pretty good. Plus the journal helps me remember what I was thinking and what we were doing when he said it, which is cool.

But on the days where I actually just wanted to talk to him, it's not enough. That's what I was feeling when I was waiting for his call that might not even happen.

Grandpa could tell I was getting antsy and upset, but he didn't say anything.

My homework was done.

I'd taken a shower.

I'd already helped wash and dry the stuff Grandpa

said we couldn't put in the dishwasher.

All my regular chores were done. Houseplants watered. Bed made. Laundry folded. Tiberius fed.

When I first moved in, Grandpa asked if I ever took the trash out. I told him Dad always took it out. And then when he raised an eyebrow, I explained that the bag was always too heavy with the bottles in it. He didn't say anything about the trash after that.

Now all that was left was that hour before bedtime.

Because now I have a bedtime.

Before I lived with Grandpa, I'd just fall asleep while Dad played his guitar. Sometimes it was at eight, sometimes it was at ten thirty. Dad never really cared about stuff like bedtimes, but even though he doesn't do routine like Grandpa, he *can* be predictable. Like we never did anything just because it was a Tuesday, but if Dad and I ever walked by a bakery, we were going in.

If he is ever close enough to a dandelion, he picks it right away and blows all the fluff off because he never thinks of it as blowing weeds into someone else's yard like Grandpa does.

He only ever wears Converse sneakers.

He drinks his coffee black.

He always said I love you when he dropped me off for school.

So there are surprises. Lots of them. But I always know what Dad would do under any circumstance.

And I've never wondered if he loved me.

I mean, I know Grandpa loves me too—I know that—but he doesn't say it.

He says, "You got lunch money?" instead.

Still, it made me sad then, not talking to Dad.

And sometimes when I'm sad, I remember other sad things. It's like how when you're sick, all you want to do is watch old movies.

It's kinda like your sadness remembers what you did the last time you were sad and tries to do it again.

I remember Dad dropping me off at Grandpa's with all my stuff.

I remember that he didn't look like Dad then. He looked like some other guy who was pretending he wasn't nervous. It was weird because Dad never pretended to be anything other than Dad.

He was rubbing his hands together and making small talk and asking Grandpa questions about the house and then it got quiet, because both me and Grandpa knew that Dad didn't care about the house.

Dad didn't ask questions about stuff that he didn't care about unless he was avoiding something.

But I didn't know what he was avoiding.

"I'll be back as soon as I can," he'd said.

And I didn't want to cry, so I kinda just looked down.

"Hey, Walter, look at me, buddy."

I looked up because he never called me buddy. That was something strangers did. And he knew he'd screwed up by saying it. Like he was trying to act normal, and he'd just said one of the least normal things he could have said.

"I love you," he said finally. "I'll be back as soon as I can."

Anyway, tonight Grandpa tapped his fingertips on his armchair and looked up at the clock. He'd just looked at it three seconds earlier, but he looked again and then lifted himself out of his seat and walked toward the weird ceramic cat my dad made when he was, like, eight or something. It hung from the wall and had a tail that curled out that Grandpa used for hanging his keys.

"Let's go," he said.

"Where are we going?" I asked.

"We're going for a drive. You don't have to change. We're not getting out."

I didn't understand.

Grandpa did routines. He didn't leave the house after dinner, ever. And I was already in my PJ pants. And it was a school night.

This was not routine.

This was really weird.

Tiberius was annoyed when I stood up and plopped him on his fuzzy pink pillow, but I got into my grandpa's truck and we started driving.

We drove past all the regular old-people stops.

The vet where he takes Tiberius once in a while.

The library.

The post office.

But those are daytime places, and it was already dark, so I wasn't sure where we were going.

We took a sharp left turn after the post office and started climbing a hill for what felt like ten minutes straight.

I wanted to ask where we were going and what we were doing here on this hill covered with trees and bushes.

But I didn't because it was the first time in a while that I remembered that my grandpa was my dad's dad.

This was exactly the kind of thing Dad would do.

I didn't say a word the whole ride. I was afraid that Grandpa would be able to hear how much I missed Dad.

Sometimes it gave me a stomachache.

So I just kept watching the road ahead get windier and windier until it finally flattened out next to a wooden post that read Apple Creek Hiking Trail.

Grandpa pulled into a parking spot and turned off the truck.

"You coming?" he asked as he opened his door and stepped out.

"You said we weren't getting out," I said.

"I meant we're not leaving the truck."

I unbuckled my seat belt, and I felt the truck bounce as Grandpa climbed onto the tailgate.

He waved at me, and I got out.

"I used to bring your dad here when he was small," he said. "He liked to look at the stars."

I waited for him to keep talking, but he just pulled two ice cream sandwiches out of his coat pocket and handed me one. They were a little soft but still good.

I looked up at the sky and felt small. In a good way, though. It was like the sky had cracked open and the stars had spilled everywhere.

Dad would have talked to me about school or pulled out his guitar, but Grandpa didn't say anything. Dad probably would have said that Grandpa was letting the stars do the talking.

It was cold, but I didn't want to go into the truck and grab the plaid jacket I knew Grandpa kept back there, because I knew if I moved from that spot everything would be over.

So I shivered a little bit and ate my ice cream, and even though I still missed Dad, I could tell that I wasn't the only one who missed him.

Even if it was deep down for Grandpa.

Maybe he misses Dad when he was small and doesn't really miss him now like I do.

But at least we both missed him.

FOUR

I'D BEEN AT APPLE Grove a week when I realized my French accent needed work.

Oui! *It definitely does*, Dad would have said, in a perfect French accent.

You Americans have no respect for French cuisine. With your French fries and cheeesebuuurgas. 'Ow dare you!

I laughed and imagined Dad brushing his teeth and winking at me.

Best of luck with your audition, old bean.

He would have switched to a British accent to say that.

"Walter," Grandpa called from downstairs.

"Coming," I shouted back.

We both live close enough to walk, but Grandpa and Fil's mom both dropped us off early the next morning for school. Usually, Grandpa just drives through the drop-off line and waves, but today we were early enough that there were spots out front. We pulled in next to the bright yellow kindergarten classroom. Fil's mom pulled right in next to us in her emerald-green minivan. Fil and I both got out.

"Hey," said Fil.

"Hey," I said back.

Fil put her hand over her face as her mom raced around her car to talk to Grandpa.

"Sorry," Fil said. "Mom will talk to anything. My sister says that's how our cactus died."

I was about to tell Fil I didn't think her mom killed a cactus by talking to it too much, but then I heard my grandpa say, "I think that would be okay." He waved me over.

"Do you want to have dinner over at your friend's house tonight?"

It was one of those social things Grandpa doesn't really pay much attention to. Like, you aren't really supposed to ask that question in front of the person asking you to do something. He was supposed to do it in secret to give me the chance to say no.

"Sure," I said. Because luckily, I wanted to go.

"Great!" said Fil's mom. "I'll pick them both up after auditions."

"Auditions?" Grandpa asked.

"For *Willy Wonka*!" said Fil's mom in a super-loud, high-pitched, super-excited voice.

"I didn't know you wanted to be in a play," Grandpa said, looking at me.

"I don't," I said, shaking my head.

"We'll see," said Fil.

Then suddenly someone honked a horn, which made us all jump.

It was coming from Fil's car.

"Mom! I'm going to be late."

Sarabeth has wavy hair like Fil's too, but it was tied back in two long braids that fell over her shoulders. You could only tell it was actually curly because of the inch of twirly hair at the bottom that looked like fusilli pasta.

"Sarabeth, if you honk that horn one more time—"

Fil's mom didn't finish her threat as she jumped back in the car after wishing us luck.

Sarabeth is in sixth grade at Apple Grove Middle School across the street. She still gets dropped off there in the morning, right after Fil. For some reason this makes Fil laugh.

"She wants to walk, but Mom insists." She shrugs. "And for the record, my mom named us both after our grandmothers, in case you're wondering why we both have old-people names."

I didn't bother telling her that Walter was an old-person name too.

Grandpa looked me over and said he'd come pick me up at Fil's around seven thirty. I watched his truck roll down the street and then disappear around the corner back to his house. I wondered, briefly, what he was going to do until he came to get me.

We walked through the front gate, and Fil made a weird face at a group of girls sitting in a circle playing a clapping game I will never understand.

The girl with the pink hair streak was Megan. The girl with the neon green backpack and bright white tennis shoes was Mona. And the girl with the long brown hair down to her waist was Rachel.

Fil deliberately turned in the opposite direction.

"Not your friends?" I asked.

"Nope," she said. "C'mon, I'll walk you to the office."

I thought it was weird that Fil would walk away from anyone, and I was going to ask her about it until we got to the front office.

The old ladies behind the front desk treated me like I was a bad smell, so I think it's pretty clear that they don't like that I'm doing morning announcements. Mrs. Butte put the recorder on her desk like she was handing it over to me even though she didn't really want to.

"Mrs. Butte doesn't like kids," Fil whispered to me. "She's one of those grown-ups who are cranky for no reason. My mom even tried to cheer her up one day because that's what my mom does with everyone, and Mrs. Butte asked her if there was somewhere she needed to be."

I wasn't allowed to start the morning announcements until Mrs. Butte handed me the mic, and this morning she took her sweet time stacking papers and clearing her desk, then smoothing her dress to stand up before she gestured to the seat I'd be sitting in.

"I know last time you got *creative*," she said. "But this time, just read the announcements." Then she looked at Fil. "Shouldn't you be heading to class?"

When her high heels clip-clopped away, Fil rolled her eyes and said she'd see me later.

The front office was weirdly quiet with no one else there. I imagined my dad clearing his throat and making that hollow sound that happens when he taps his guitar right before he starts playing. Then I started wondering what he was doing and shook my head.

I didn't really want to think about that—not right now.

Instead, I watched the clock until it was time to start reading.

I was all set to do the alien thing again because Mrs. Pudumjee said she liked it. Actually, she never said she liked it, but she did ask if Trox could come back, so I assumed that meant she liked it.

But then I saw the sheet of paper, and I didn't really want to do the alien voice again.

I scribbled out a few lines and wrote some other notes down around the margins of the paper.

The clock ticked to eight o'clock, and another voice took over.

My dad does a lot of funny voices too. Cartoon voices mostly, but sometimes he does impressions.

And the one that always makes me laugh is when he pretends to be Queen Elizabeth.

I pressed the blue button.

Good morning, students of Apple Grove Performing Arts Academy.

This is Her Royal Majesty Queen Elizabeth II.

Please do pay attention as I read your announcements for Monday, January twenty-first, 2019.

This week's lunch specials shall be a loaded baked potato—loaded with what precisely is unclear—macaroni and cheese, chicken noodle casserole, and bean and cheese burritos.

I am told this is all American food you will heartily enjoy.

Kids were laughing in their classrooms. Louder than they did when I was an alien. I thought Dad would be laughing too, so I kept going in my English old lady voice. It wasn't really the Queen's voice because I didn't know what she actually sounded like.

Student Council will be selling sweets this week to raise money for our second vegetable garden between the third and fourth grade classrooms.

How lovely.

The final selections for the spring production of Willy Wonka and the Chocolate Factory *shall be posted outside Mr. Thibodo's door tomorrow afternoon.*

Thank you for your attention.

Her Royal Highness, signing off.

I'd changed the word "lollypops" to "sweets" and was feeling pretty proud of myself as I clicked the blue button again and listened to everyone outside laughing.

"Nice work," said Mrs. Pudumjee, who was standing behind me.

"Sometimes it's just fun to pretend to be someone else for a while," I told her.

That's my line, Dad would have said.

Dad says that all the time. He says it's a relief to pretend for a while because it gives you a break from being yourself.

Plus, it seemed like something Dad would do. Something he'd like. After Mrs. Pudumjee left, I pulled out the journal and flipped to a random page.

At some point, you are going to need someone to tell you when your breath stinks. When you have a booger. When your shirt is tucked into your underwear. You're going to need someone to look at you and tell you you're gross so that you don't go out into the world with your grossness.

I was still holding the journal when I walked out into the hall and noticed that Fil was waiting. Actually, she was doing a handstand, and she kicked down into a bridge and crab-walked toward me.

"Thought you went to class already," I said.

"Mrs. Pudumjee said I could wait for you, Your Majesty. What's that?"

I told her about writing down all the stuff Dad said in the orange journal, and I showed her the part I just read.

She laughed.

"It would be an honor to tell you when you're gross, Wally."

Then we walked to class on two legs, even though Fil would've rather gone on her hands.

FIVE

TODAY'S ORANGE JOURNAL ENTRY:

There are a lot of reasons to stay inside and never leave. Humans are mostly terrible. But the one reason you should always get out if you can is that nothing will really happen if you don't leave. And someone might need you. Your voice. Your story. Your smile. Even a dirty look or the middle finger they deserve in traffic.

The theater at Apple Grove has those fold-down seats with maroon velvet. They all squeak. There's a plaque at the front of the stage with a bunch of names of all the rich people who donated money to build it or something. Plus, the place has the faint smell of wood polish.

Everything looks like how an actual theater should look. Like one for real actors, not just kids, which is why I guess it makes sense that Mr. Thibodo takes auditions seriously. It isn't a school play to him. It's just Way-Off Broadway.

And because Mr. Thibodo treats it so seriously, everyone else does too. It was pretty quiet in the auditorium except for the sound of people practicing their scales or trying to decide what song to sing.

Fil and I sat down. She shuffled through her backpack, pulled out a candy bar, and then started humming to herself.

"Getting into character," she said with chocolate in her teeth. "You sure you don't want to give it a try?"

"I'm sure," I said.

Fil brushed the hair out of her eyes with one hand and twitched her foot.

She was one of the first people to be called.

And she was good.

Like, really good.

She even nailed the best line from the best song. *DON'T CARE HOW. I WANT IT NOW.*

Everyone laughed, even Mr. Thibodo.

"Very nice, Ms. Garfield," he said.

Travis Talbert went next, and he didn't suck nearly as much as I'd hoped he would.

Then a bunch of girls went up and said they wanted to be Oompa Loompas, but not orange. And wow. They were really good.

There was a moment when they all screamed in perfect harmony and the sound was so powerful that all the hair on my body stood up. Their Oompa Loompa song about Augustus Gloop was the best thing I'd heard all day, but I wouldn't have said that anywhere near Fil.

When it was over and people were getting ready to go home, Mr. Thibodo turned around and said—

"Announcement Kid. You're up."

I actually looked around.

"Oh, I'm not on the list," I said.

"I wasn't asking if you were on the list. I was telling you you're up."

He pushed his glasses up his nose and didn't look away.

I looked over at Fil, who was looking smug.

"Just do it," she whispered. "Half the people are gone. If you suck, no one will know."

"Thanks," I said.

"You won't suck," she added quickly.

I stood in the center of the stage. It was super quiet. A few people came back into the auditorium, I think because someone went out and told them that Announcement Kid was going up.

"Whenever you're ready..."

I was sweating a little. I knew every scene by heart so I had options, but there was still that moment of panic when I realized that I was doing this in front of people.

I'd never asked Dad about that, about how to pretend you're brave.

That's when I decided to go for my dad's favorite part with Willy Wonka. The part where he goes nuts on the boat.

"There's no earthly way of knowing," I said.

Silence.

"Which direction we are going."

Silence.

"There's no knowing where we're rowing

Or which way the river's flowing," I sang.

It's not really the kind of song you sing, though.

It's like sing-talking. And by the time I got to the last few words, I was really missing Dad, so I was glad it was over when it was over.

Dad had this whole part memorized, so I wasn't so much acting as I was doing my impression of Dad doing his impression of Gene Wilder, the actor who played Willy Wonka in the original movie.

And it's strange because as I stood there pretending to be Willy Wonka leading all the kids onstage on a super creepy boat ride through his factory, I knew a bunch of kids were going to think I was a total weirdo. The version I know, the Gene Wilder version, is a really old movie. Like from the '70s or something. And I know it's been redone, but the old version is the one Dad loves.

It was like the soundtrack to our life, and the only thing we had in the car for entertainment when we were heading to Grandpa's house from Michigan, so it was still pretty fresh in my brain.

I remember Dad was tired from all the driving, but at night in whatever motel we'd stopped at, he'd bust out Willy Wonka. I'd watch with him on his laptop because even though I'd already seen it a million times, it wasn't boring doing it with Dad. It wasn't boring doing anything with Dad.

When I was done, Fil was grinning with her arms crossed. A big stupid smile on her face because she was about to tell me I told you so.

Not in a mean way. But I knew she couldn't wait to say it.

Then I started to walk offstage, and Mr. Thibodo called me back.

"Hey, um—" He whispered to Fil, I think because he wanted to call me by my real name but didn't know it. I heard her tell him who I was.

"Walter, you got another song? Something you can actually sing."

Mr. Thibodo pressed the tips of his fingers together and looked at me. Fil looked at me too, but I think she was trying to talk to me with her eyes.

But I didn't want to do that. I wanted to be in my own head.

I'd seen Dad do it onstage hundreds of times. He always closed his eyes. Just for a second. So I imagined what he'd say.

Then I'm not nervous, Walter. Because for a second it's just me and the song, and I can be anywhere I want.

So I sang "Pure Imagination."

It's from the part in the movie where Willy Wonka takes all the kids who won the contest to see the room in his factory where *everything* is made of candy. He has this moment where he tries to teach them to follow their dreams even though no one is really listening, they just want to eat the candy rocks and gummy bears as big as their faces.

I forgot I was singing for people while I did it. I think I did a pretty good job because everyone who stayed behind to watch applauded.

Mr. Thibodo leaned back in his chair and twirled his pen in his hand.

"Very nice, Walter."

"Don't crowd him," Fil said when I got offstage. I laughed, and she nudged me in the shoulder. "C'mon," she said. "Mom's waiting. Oh, and just so you know, it's my turn to ride in the front, so if you think for one second that I'm going to miss a chance to kick Sarabeth out of that seat just because you're riding with us, you are mistaken."

Fil liked saying that a lot. *You're mistaken.* Or *that's false.* Or *correct, but just barely.*

I didn't tell her it wasn't just her name that made her sound like a grandma.

Fil's mom asked us immediately how auditions went once we got close enough to the car. Sarabeth sighed, audibly.

"Mom, it's just a fifth-grade play," she said, rolling her eyes.

"Mom," said Fil. "Sarabreath is in my seat."

Fil grinned at Sarabeth as she unclicked her seat belt, letting it smack into the car door with a loud clang as she climbed through the back of the minivan to sit next to me.

"I thought for sure you'd want to sit with Walter," Fil's mom said.

Fil looked back at me.

"He's fine," she said. "And rehearsals were awesome. WE were awesome."

That's another thing about Fil. If you're her friend and you do something good, she will tell everybody.

I don't know if it's weird that I've never had dinner at a friend's house, but until tonight, I hadn't.

Fil's mom made chicken and rice and pan-fried zucchini. And Fil and Sarabeth had their own seats with their own place mats.

"Ugh, Mom, I don't need my fifty states place mat anymore, okay? Sixth grade, remember?" Sarabeth pushed a piece of hair out of her face and rolled her eyes.

"Sorry, honey, just swap it out," Fil's mom said, putting a spoon into the rice cooker.

Then Fil rolled her eyes too.

"She used to fight me for that one," Fil said. She said it in a whisper, but she seemed to also be saying it just loud enough so Sarabeth could hear.

"Shut up, turd rocket," Sarabeth whispered.

"You shut up, butthole," Fil said back.

But she wasn't as quiet as Sarabeth.

"Filomena!" Fil's mom shouted. "Don't you dare talk that way to your sister."

"But, Mom, I was just—"

"No buts," said Fil's mom. She'd already turned her attention back to the zucchini. "Why don't you show Walter around? Dinner will be ready in ten."

"She never catches Sarabeth," Fil said, shaking her head as she led me up the stairs. A framed collage of puppy pictures was on the door.

"Mom says we can get a dog if we both stay on

the honor roll all year," said Fil. Then she opened the door, and the first thing I noticed was that the room was, like, super clean.

I was going to ask her about it, but she just looked at me like she knew what I was gonna say.

"Sarabeth is a slob."

Then I understood.

I looked around at the walls she'd covered in animal posters. Her shelves were filled with books that had animals all over the covers. Koalas seemed to be her favorite.

"Dad always wanted to be a vet when he was a kid," she said. "These were his."

"So, you want to be a vet because your dad wants you to be?" I asked.

"Is that why you do voices?" Fil asked.

"No, Dad doesn't care about that."

"So why do you do voices, then?" Fil raised an eyebrow.

"I don't know," I lied.

I definitely do voices because of Dad.

But maybe that's okay as long as I like it?

Fil had an exercise ball in the corner of her room next to a small trampoline and a yoga mat.

"When's he supposed to be back from his gig?" Fil asked. She did a handstand against her bedroom door while I sat at her desk.

I shrugged.

"Has he ever left you behind before?"

"Nope," I said.

She nodded.

"Well, there's probably a good reason why this time is different," she said, landing back on her feet.

And she's probably right. Fil is smart. Not in an annoying know-it-all way. She reads people pretty quickly. She can tell what kind of person someone is with only a few details. She also doesn't talk about stuff she doesn't know anything about, like talking just to sound smart.

But . . .

Telling someone that there's probably a good reason their dad ditched them is not really what any kid wants to hear.

I think she could tell that's what I was thinking, because she changed the subject.

"Alrighty then, you should practice. You do some voices, and I'll tell you who they are."

So we did.

Goofy.

Yoda.

President Obama.

"That was awesome. You sound just like him," Fil said. "What else ya got?"

Then there was one she couldn't get.

"Who is that one?" she asked.

"What? Seriously?" I said.

Dad had always said it was easily my best impression. The one voice that everyone would get right away, no matter what, but Fil looked confused.

"Are you just practicing your British accent?" she said.

"Have you never watched *Star Trek: The Next Generation*?" I said.

She shook her head, and I was shocked.

"It's Captain Picard."

When she looked at me blankly again, I went over to her computer and pulled up a clip of the show. We watched a bald British guy in a red Starfleet uniform start the most famous speech of the series:

Space: the final frontier. These are the voyages of the starship Enterprise.

Fil listened for a few minutes, then watched five seconds of an episode.

"Oh yeah. Professor Xavier from X-Men."

"I just can't with you right now," I said.

We spent a while arguing about why she should know exactly who Sir Patrick Stewart is, and after a few more YouTube videos, she finally admitted that my Captain Picard voice is really good, but she said not to use it for the morning announcements, because no one would know who I was supposed to be.

"You could probably do Professor X, though. Same voice, but you'll need to tell them who you are."

"That means it's not good enough on its own," I grumbled. Fil laughed. "Does Sarabeth want a dog too?" I asked.

Fil rolled her eyes. "Yes, a Labradoodle."

"What's wrong with—"

"Nothing if you're completely boring and don't want to actually rescue a dog."

Then she spun off into an annoyed rant about puppy mills (places they build puppies, maybe?) and dogs at the pound, and how her family should get an older dog *and* a younger dog and how she was going to convince her parents to let her do this.

"Anyway, that's why I want to be a vet. I want to have a bunch of animals."

"Um. You can do that without becoming a vet. You know that, right?" She was definitely about to roll her eyes at me when she had a completely random thought that sort of bubbled out of her.

"Ohmygosh, can you do Ursula's voice from *Little Mermaid*?"

For the next twenty minutes, I practiced talking like a half-octopus woman who definitely was once a smoker. We kept at it until Fil said my impression was perfect.

"She is my favorite villain," Fil said.

I was about to tell her that she'd clearly forgotten Cruella De Vil when her mom called us from downstairs.

"Filomena! Sarabeth! Walter! Dinner!"

We really do have old-people names, I thought.

We all bolted from the bedrooms and made it to the landing at the top of the stairs at the same time. Sarabeth dove for the railing and slid down first.

I'm not sure why this bothered Fil, but it did. Everything about her sister seemed to bother Fil.

When we got downstairs, Fil's dad was kissing Fil's mom in a really gross, obvious way.

"Ewww! Mom, please!" Fil said.

Fil's mom laughed, and Fil's dad said, "Hey, Curly, is this Walter?"

He put his hand out to shake mine.

"Fil says you do voices."

He smiled, and even though he was nice and friendly and I could tell Fil loved him, I knew right away he wasn't the sort of guy who would be friends with my dad. He dressed like a regular dad coming home from work. He was a little fatter than my dad. Had less hair, seemed tired—

He looked, I think, like dads are supposed to look.

But mainly I think it was the way he talked that would have put my dad off.

Some people have a voice that they use in public or for strangers and they save their real voice for at home, and I could tell Fil's dad was using his "stranger voice" for me. My dad doesn't have a stranger voice. He talks to everybody the same.

So I did my *Star Trek* Captain Jean-Luc Picard voice because it's something Dad would have done if he wasn't sure about someone.

And Fil's dad laughed a big, loud, real laugh from his belly.

"I love *Star Trek*," he said, still smiling.

I guess he's okay too.

Grandpa picked me up at seven thirty on the dot. Fil's mom walked us out to the car with cookies, talking about the play and the school and the kids and how great it was that Fil and I were friends.

"Mom . . ." Fil said with her face in her hands.

Then we got into the car and pulled out of the driveway, and it was quiet.

Quieter than it had been for hours.

"She likes to talk," Grandpa said.

"Yep," I said.

That night Dad called.

And here's what I don't get.

I'd been thinking about him practically all day. Imagining how I'd tell him about the play and the audition and everything. But when I picked up the phone to talk to him, I was mad.

I think it was because Dad asked the question as if he hadn't forgotten to call the last few days. As if everything was normal, and for some reason, I was mad about that. I didn't want to pretend like everything was okay. And I didn't want to tell him stories about my day. I just wanted to be mad.

So I said *fine*. Just *fine*.

I didn't ask about Dad's day. I knew he wouldn't answer. We never talked about where he was. And it's not that I didn't want to know where he was playing music or what town he was in. I just didn't wanna talk about it. I didn't want to think about how much time it was going to be before I saw him again. And I didn't want him to wonder if maybe I was too much trouble and if maybe he didn't want to come back. And I knew it was probably a bad idea to stay mad. Because who wants to come back to someone who's mad at them?

But still when he asked me what was going on at school, I said, "Nothing. Nothing, really."

Normally I'm good at details.

What I had for lunch.

What I read.

But I just said, "Nothing. Nothing, really."

Nothing about lunch. Nothing about Fil. I didn't tell him about the audition. Or about the song. I just told him Grandpa made beef stew for dinner. Then I asked when he was coming home when I should've said when are you coming to Grandpa's because we really didn't have a home anymore, not together anyway.

And that's how I knew Dad was going to cut the conversation short. But this time it wasn't him doing it, it was me.

You can still love somebody and be mad at them. You can still miss somebody and be mad at them. Being mad at somebody doesn't mean anything.

But sometimes it makes you remember other stuff that you're mad at them for.

Like when Dad forgot to sign a permission slip for a field trip, and I had to stay behind while the rest of my class went to the zoo.

It wasn't my worst day at school. I watched movies all day, but when I got home, my dad was asleep on the couch and I couldn't even nudge him awake. I told him when he woke up, and he took me to the zoo on a school day because he felt so bad that I missed the field trip.

"Nothing at all happened?" Dad asked again. I tried to picture where he was, and what kind of room he'd be in that would echo like that. Like he was talking to me from inside a bathroom.

"Nope. Just a boring day," I said. Then there was silence on the phone for a second. Nobody hates silence more than Dad.

"Oh," he said. "Well, that's okay. They can't all be awesome, right?" he said. And it hurt. That moment. Dad trying to be nice and me being a jerk. Even though I couldn't stop myself.

He told me about a new song he was writing and asked a little bit more about Grandpa, and we hung up.

Two seconds later, Fil called.

"Wally," she said seriously. For a minute, I thought somebody died.

"What?"

"Did you check your email?"

I don't check my email every day. Especially since I never had an email address before starting at Apple Grove.

"Nope," I said.

"Mr. Thibodo posted the cast of the play on the school website. You're Willy Wonka!"

"That's awesome," I said, and I meant it. I really

did. I'd never been in a play before, so this was huge and I was excited to talk to Fil about it, but the person I really wanted to talk to was Dad and he wasn't there and I didn't know where he was and I couldn't even call him back.

"Are you sure? You sound . . . not jazzed," Fil said.

"I'm really excited!" I said. "Just tired, sorry. I can't believe I'm Wonka."

"God, I wish I could be the one to tell Buttcream."

She'd started calling Travis Buttcream during PE. Not to his face—just to me when she knew no one else could hear.

"First rehearsal is tomorrow," said Fil. "Sleep tight, Wally."

"You too," I said.

Fil was the first person I'd ever said good night to over the phone besides Dad. And there was something kinda . . . I dunno about that.

But part of me wished I could call Dad back because I wanted to know what he would say when he found out.

That movie is our thing. And yes, I know it was a book first.

Because Fil already did that eye roll thing that

people do where they just assume that because there's a book it is automatically BETTER than the movie.

And the book is good. No doubt. But, like, it doesn't really give you that level of shock that SEEING AUGUSTUS GLOOP SUCKED UP AN ACTUAL PIPE does, you know? Or, like, that scene where Veruca sings a full song about being a brat and getting everything she wants before being sent down the garbage chute to the incinerator. When I first saw it, I didn't even know that they burned trash. I had to ask Dad what "incinerate" means.

The movie was a huge part of us, you know? It was the thing we always turned on when we needed background noise, because for a while we didn't have much. Most of what we owned fit in the trunk of a car, so when you don't have a lot, the stuff you *do* have becomes way more important.

So I guess I had to think about how I felt for a minute because Willy Wonka for me was always my dad. He's weird, and not everybody gets him. He makes inappropriate jokes about tragic accidents.

So when you watch a character who reminds you of somebody that you miss, it's a little bit weird when somebody asks you to play that character. It makes you miss them more. At least that's what happened with me. I wanted so bad to tell Dad about my day. I wanted to tell him about Grandpa and about how Tiberius is the size of a raccoon and how is it even possible for a cat to be that huge? And I guess, more than anything, I just want Dad to be around. So that's why I always look in the orange journal and pretend it's magic. Because it reminds me that he's still somewhere even if I don't know where.

But the orange journal is definitely not magic, because this is the entry I flipped open:

> You're not rich if you have a favorite pair of underwear.

SIX

IT'S SUNDAY, AND THAT means Donut Day.

Grandpa only goes to one donut shop, Donut Holes.

And he only ever gets one thing. A glazed old-fashioned buttermilk.

I can't get the same thing every time.

Sometimes I grab a jelly donut.

Sometimes a cinnamon roll.

Chocolate long Johns are awesome too.

It's always the same old guys who hang out there. And they're always doing the same thing—talking, eating donuts, and watching who comes through the door.

The shop has a door with a little bell on it, and the tables are small and square with chairs that make a loud squeaking noise every time they're pushed in and out, which isn't often with old people. Which is probably a good thing, as the guys that come in generally park their butts in those chairs for hours.

On the wall there's a bulletin board of flyers with lost dogs and stuff. But at the top is a laminated newspaper clipping of Dad on *Hometown Tunes* and another one just below it about his song being played on the local radio station.

Grandpa glances over at it every time we walk in.

We ate our donuts at a small table for two in the corner. He drank his coffee, and I drank my milk out of a little blue carton with a farm girl on it.

"Why didn't you tell your dad about the play?"

"I found out I got Wonka after he called," I said.

"Yeah, but you didn't mention the play at all before that."

I shrugged. I could tell Grandpa had been waiting until Donut Day to ask me because it's easier to ask big questions when the other person is eating donuts.

Still, Grandpa didn't say anything after I shrugged. He's not the kind of grown-up who forces you to talk when you don't want to.

"I know you miss him," Grandpa said. "But he'll be home soon."

"He's never left me for work before. He promised he never would," I said. I knew I sounded like a baby, but I didn't care. I ate around the chocolate on my donut.

Grandpa didn't say anything else as we got back in his truck, and I didn't ask any more questions. I don't want to be the kind of person who forces someone to talk when they don't want to, either.

Grandpa is retired from a lot of stuff. When my dad was in high school, Grandpa retired from the marines as a colonel. Then he got a job working for the city, and while he was doing that, he worked part-time with my grandma at a cat rescue place, which he still says was NOT his idea. Retired marine. Retired city worker. Retired cat guy.

For a while the only thing I couldn't figure out about Grandpa was Tiberius.

Grandpa says he hates cats. And I'm pretty sure he's also allergic. But Dad said he had a cat when he was growing up too, and now he has Tiberius, a massive pumpkin-sized cat who has his own pink fluffy pillow.

But my grandma loved cats, and that was it.

That's how they got Tiberius when he was a kitten. Now Tiberius is old and fat and just wants to lie in the sun. He is about my age, because my grandparents adopted him just before I was born, which is around the same time my grandma died. I never met her, but Grandpa says she was really excited when Dad told her I was on my way.

So I think that's why the routine and keeping busy thing is important to him. He doesn't want his brain to get a rest so he has to think about stuff that bothers him.

He doesn't want to miss anybody else, and I think maybe he doesn't want to worry about being somebody that someone else might miss.

It's complicated.

"What if we did rock climbing?" he asked, completely out of nowhere, even though he'd probably been trying to say it for a while.

"Like . . . outside?" I asked.

It wasn't fishing or hunting or stamp collecting or anything else a grandpa might do, so it could have been a lot worse, but I still couldn't figure out why rock climbing.

He shoved a brochure at me from his gym.

RACE TO THE TOP

*Grab a partner and find your way
up black diamond ridge!*

"We don't have to do the competition," he said quickly. "But they just finished building the indoor wall at the gym, and they gave a bunch of members five free climbs with a partner, so I thought . . ."

I held the last bite of my donut between my fingers and looked at him.

"Okay," I said.

"Okay," he said. "Good."

Dad called later that afternoon, and before I could get caught up in missing him, I said, "Guess who just got the lead in *Willy Wonka and the Chocolate Factory*?"

And as I told him about the audition and Fil and Mr. Thibodo, I could hear his smile through the phone.

SEVEN

Why is a yawn contagious? Even thinking about a yawn makes me yawn. Now I'm yawning.

WHEN I GOT TO school, Fil wasn't there, which was weird because Fil is never late. That's her thing. It's what she's known for. I knew she'd probably be out for the rest of the day. Being sick is the only thing that would keep her from Apple Grove.

So I just sat in our usual spot and watched all the other weirdos arrive.

It's kinda nice being at a place where everyone is weird. I mean everyone everywhere IS weird anyway, like even outside Apple Grove. They just pretend they're not.

At Apple Grove you can put on mismatched socks or shave part of your head or sing Christmas carols in February, and nobody cares.

Seriously, nobody cares. I think that's the most amazing thing about art school. Everything that makes people look at you funny in the real world gets zero reaction from anyone here. Because however weird you are, it's not enough.

Blue hair? Whatever.

You walk on your hands? Cool. Just wash them before you eat.

Memorized your favorite rap song in a different language? Yawn.

It's nice practice for when people might pay you to be weird. 'Cuz that's what the school is secretly hoping. That some of us go on to be weird professionally, because Grandpa says the minute somebody pays you for doing something kooky, you become an "artist."

He always puts "artist" in air quotes like it's a make-believe word.

That's not what they say here, though. They say you're an artist when you close your eyes and think of something that didn't exist before you thought of it.

Like a song or a picture or a performance, I guess.

But Grandpa doesn't like that because he says that makes everyone an artist. I don't tell him that's kinda the point, because he'd just roll his eyes.

Then the bell rang, and I didn't want to walk into the office to do morning announcements without Fil, but I didn't really have a choice either.

The front office had just cracked the doors open. I could tell because the old ladies looked annoyed that a kid was already in there.

The office ladies weren't like anyone else at Apple Grove. Every other teacher I'd met was over-the-top nice and super happy to be there. Whereas these two kinda wrinkled their noses every time a kid walked in front of them.

We can't all stink.

When it was time to press the button and start the announcements, I remembered the last one Fil said she really liked, but it was a long shot. Not everybody knew this voice. So I had to cheat a little. Just a little.

AND I, JACK, THE PUMPKIN KING,

Would like to read you this morning's announcements . . .

The Nightmare Before Christmas is a classic, but it's also creepy. Like, I'm not sure why anyone ever thought it was a good idea to make a children's movie about a dead skeleton guy capturing Santa and ruining Christmas. But there it is.

"Hey, Jack!" When I didn't turn around, the same kid yelled, "Jack Skellington!" So I finally understood he meant me.

I turned around and realized it was a kid I recognized from auditions. He had short brown locs that he flung away from his forehead when he talked.

"Tetherball," he said. He pointed to the tetherball court, and I nodded.

For recess you run to wherever you're going. No one walks to pick up their jump rope or handball, and definitely no one walks to get in line for tetherball. Jamal is the kid who called me over. The other kids, a redhead with freckles named Sam and a Vietnamese kid with two skinned knees and a scrape across his knuckles named William, all got in line behind me.

We didn't really talk much, but when the bell rang, Jamal told me to sit with them at lunch.

It still felt funny that Fil wasn't there, and just as I was thinking about how she'd probably be reciting some lines from TV if she were there, a girl walked past our table. I recognized her from the group Fil avoided. "I'm Rachel," she said. "You sit with Fil all the time."

"Yeah," I said.

"She's a weirdo," Rachel told me in a whisper before walking off.

"Um. Okay," I said. It was weird thing to say at the lunch tables to someone you didn't really know. And it sounded like she talked like that a lot.

"Rachel hates Fil," Jamal said, taking a bite of his sandwich before tossing his juice in the trash.

"How can anyone hate Fil?" I asked.

"Girl stuff, I guess." Jamal shrugged.

But it was super weird, so I asked Fil about it the next day when she was back at school after being out sick.

"Never," she said dramatically, "be the first one to fall asleep at a slumber party." When I just stared at her, she added, "My mom made me go. And I fell asleep. And they put my hand in warm water. And I peed in my sleeping bag."

"Oh," I said.

"Yep."

"What did you do?" I asked.

"Well, I peed."

"After that," I said.

"I changed my underwear and waited for everyone else to fall asleep. Then I went to her cat's litter box and scooped cat poop into each of their sleeping bags."

"You what?"

"Yeah. For all the other girls at the party, I put it in their sleeping bags, but for Rachel I put it on her pillow."

I laughed and couldn't stop laughing. Fil laughed too, and we stood up when the lunch bell rang.

"Then what happened?" I asked.

"Rachel lives close to me, so I just left and walked home. Rachel's mom was mad that I left and about the cat poop everywhere and my mom was mad that I left Rachel's house in the middle of the night without Rachel's mom knowing about it because it was super dangerous and anything could have happened to me. I got grounded for a week, but my mom was actually still more mad at Rachel's mom."

"And what about Rachel?"

"She woke up with her face next to cat poop."

"But you don't act mean around her at all, even though she made you pee in front of everyone."

"Because she woke up with cat poop next to her face. I think I'm good."

I nodded. Then I thought for a second.

"Wait . . . There was enough cat poop to scoop into all their sleeping bags?"

"No, I had to break it up with the scooper. I saved the biggest pieces for Rachel, though."

So not only did Fil seek revenge in the middle of the night against Rachel, she also divided up cat poop to make sure that everyone who was a part of it was appropriately shamed henceforward. I imagined her trying to decide which girls got the bigger pieces of poop.

"That's awesome," I told her.

"I know," said Fil.

EIGHT

Life is an adventure. Or at least it should be. People don't realize when they're walking around that this is all we have. This moment. Right now. The fact that some people spend their time being bored or doing things they hate absolutely baffles me. It makes me want to hand them a waffle and take them zip-lining.

Try new stuff! It could be awesome. I mean, why not? If you suck at least there will be a good story.

I REMEMBER THAT THIS was the day Dad bought (and quickly returned) a skateboard. He fell hard and got a purple bruise covering his entire left butt cheek and talked about it for weeks after.

So, Grandpa and I were not good at rock climbing.

That's why I don't really mind doing it. I've never seen Grandpa try to do something he isn't good at before. Seeing him suck at something makes me feel less stupid.

We've actually gone a couple times since Grandpa first suggested it, and it's always the same routine. We walk into the gym wearing sweatpants and T-shirts, and the same girl with straight black hair and a nose ring hands us our ropes and walks us over to our instructor. His name is Blaine.

This is the part where Grandpa looks really uncomfortable.

Blaine is blond and super friendly. He's one of those people with a constant you-can-do-it attitude.

There is nobody more annoyed by this than Grandpa.

Not because he doesn't like positive people. I think it's because he doesn't like anyone thinking he needs help. That might be a marines thing.

We've learned how to put our harnesses on. We've learned how to tell our instructors that we were ready to climb.

We say, "On belay?" Like *ON BELL-AY?*

And they respond, "Belay on." *BELL-LAY ON*.

I always laugh at the look on Grandpa's face because I know we're both thinking, *This is stupid*, at the same time.

Even though Grandpa was in the marines, he isn't the kind of guy to say, "I was in the marines, and pretending your wall of plastic rocks is dangerous is dumb." But he was thinking it—really loud.

We climbed with Blaine between us. Even with a few lessons, we were still on the beginner side of the wall. It was marked with purple rocks. Blaine kept telling us we were doing "super" and that we were "definitely going to make it to the top someday." Grandpa clenched his teeth after five minutes of positive feedback. Then Grandpa and I both missed a step at the exact same time and face-planted into the wall.

"It's okay! It's okay! We all stumble a little when we're learning. The important thing is to get back up. C'mon, gentlemen, you can do this!"

My face was still squished into the wall a little bit, and I could feel the harness lifting my butt into the air like it was some kind of weird butt puppet. But before either of us could think of something to say to Blaine, who was now hovering enthusiastically between us, we both started laughing.

Grandpa's laugh isn't like Dad's laugh. It's deeper, and it sounds like it comes from a place that's covered by gravel and dirt and old newspaper. But when it erupts, it's strong and always makes me laugh harder.

After a few more minutes of us clamoring around the purple rocks, Blaine told us that was enough for the day. We floated to the ground by our ropes.

We both pulled a wedgie at the exact same time, as soon as our feet touched the ground.

We got back to the car, and Grandpa put the key in the ignition.

"If you don't want to go back, we don't have to. I just thought—"

He said this every time.

"I want to go back," I said quickly.

"We really don't have to."

"Yeah," I said. "I suck. But so do you, so it's kinda fun."

Then Grandpa laughed again, and we drove home.

Tiberius was watching us from the window when we pulled into the driveway.

Dad called that night, and I could tell he was in a good mood.

He told me about this song he was writing, and he asked me questions about school and the play.

"And how's Fil?" he asked. "That's your friend's name, right? The one who can walk on her hands and is playing Veruca?"

"Yeah. That's her. She's alright," I said.

Then I told him about rock climbing with Grandpa. He was quiet for a while.

"Rock climbing?"

I told him about the gym. About how Grandpa and I both sucked and then I laughed when I told him how we both face-planted into the fake mountain wall at the same time and how Grandpa hated the instructor.

It was still quiet at the other end of the phone.

"Dad?"

"That's awesome!" he said finally. "Not something I would have thought Grandpa would be into."

"He's not," I said. "He sucks. I think he just wanted to do something with me. Something fun."

"Yeah. Definitely."

Dad sounded sad. Like I'd just squashed his good mood or something. And then he was quiet, like he didn't have anything else he wanted to say. And that's how I knew the call was over.

"When are you coming to get me?" I asked.

"Soon, I hope. Love you. Talk to you tomorrow."

Then I hung up. And I thought about what I'd said.

NINE

MR. THIBODO CLAPPED HIS hands a lot. Not, like, in a specific beat or like you do when you sing "If You're Happy and You Know It." It was more of a way to get people's attention and to get them moving. Kinda like Grandpa does in the morning when he's trying to get me up for school.

In both situations, the clapping is annoying.

Mr. Thibodo's a bouncy guy too. There are times in rehearsal where he breaks us up into groups to go over our lines together. He almost hops from group to group to make sure nobody is goofing off.

Which is hard, because whenever we break off from a big group, most people just want to goof off. They wanna talk about other stuff.

"C'mon, people. Let's focus. Oompa Loompas, let's get it together."

The Oompa Loompas were all girls, except for Jamal and Pete. And it wasn't like in the old movie where they were all small and orange with green hair. They all had matching jumpsuits and gloves, but the girls were all singers at Apple Grove, so whenever they busted out a song, it was, like, awesome. And it wasn't *just* a choreographed number with people hopping over each other. It was more like a music video that told a story about kids who suck and get what they deserve.

Mr. Thibodo used all of the songs from the original movie but added a few extras.

I recognized some melodies that sounded like a blend of Beyoncé, Taylor Swift, and Michael Jackson, and I think Mr. Thibodo got some kids in creative writing to make up the lyrics.

Anyway, the Oompa Loompas sang a cappella, so without instruments, and Jamal did this amazing slow-motion break-dance thing every time they paused their song. I've never seen anyone move like that in person. Like his heart was beating out of his chest and his whole body was moving to keep up with it.

Fil looked impressed too, and I could tell she

regretted saying that I could "do better than an Oompa Loompa."

I watched them for a long time. It was easy to get lost in the way they all fit together like pieces of a machine. And I probably could have watched them for longer, but I got distracted when Travis reminded me that he was an actual person who needed me to run lines with him. He cleared his throat, and for a second, I was really jealous of Fil and Jamal and Pete and everyone else who didn't have to deal with being Willy Wonka all the time.

Travis and I were sitting in the front row of the theater where Mr. Thibodo had set up a row of folding tables for the actors who were not onstage. There were stacks of scripts lying open and a pile of Hacky Sacks that had been confiscated next to a severe-looking sign that read NO JUGGLING.

Travis looked at me like he wanted to squash my face.

He got the part he wanted, but he definitely didn't want me to be Wonka. I think if he'd had his choice, he would have picked almost anyone else to play Wonka. Maybe even a cardboard cutout.

I don't know why anyone would waste their time

being mean when they could just get over it.

One of the lines in the orange journal is something Dad says all the time:

> Mean is a lot of work. Imagine taking all that time and energy to send unpleasantness to someone else. Not only is it bad for the person on the other end, but it's awful for you too. There's a consequence for everything you do, but I think there might be one for the stuff you think too. Meanness fills you up and changes you. I honestly don't know why people bother with it.

"Let's start from here," Travis said. He liked to be in charge, and I liked to get these parts of rehearsal with him over quickly, so I let him boss me about a bit.

Travis has clearly read a lot of books on acting, which is really terrible for me, because now I have to listen to him quote those books all the time. And I already don't like Travis.

"So, we need to think about the motivation of these characters," he said.

"I think we need to think about practicing our lines," I told him.

He looked at me like I was stupid.

"That's why you're not really an actor. And I don't know why Mr. Thibodo gave you the part if you're not even going to take it seriously."

On the other side of the auditorium, Fil was practicing with all the other kids who get annihilated by the chocolate factory because they are terrible people. She was definitely having a lot more fun than I was.

Fatima, the girl playing Violet Beauregarde, was trying out her giant blueberry costume for the first time and clearly having fun walking around in it. It was inflatable, and it looked like part of it was releasing air from her butt. Everyone was laughing because she looked like a giant farting blueberry—and that's, like, one of those things in life that is always funny.

Meanwhile, I had to listen to Travis tell me about the sacred craft of acting. I wanted to barf.

Then Mr. Thibodo walked by to check in on our progress, and Travis didn't act like a know-it-all jerk-face in front of him. Probably because Mr. Thibodo actually knows stuff.

Mr. Thibodo was an actor on some TV shows in the '80s. Then he did a couple movies before he started performing on Broadway.

He got a Tony once, which is a huge deal.

Then he retired and moved away from New York City.

But he got super bored being retired, so he got a job teaching acting here at Apple Grove.

So now, every time he opens his mouth, Travis shuts his. Which makes me wish Mr. Thibodo would just talk forever.

Fil told me that one time there was this kid who told his friend that he thought Thibodo was a loser because he just *taught* theater and didn't *do* theater, and Mr. Thibodo heard him. And he didn't even bring up his Tony. He just laughed like a supervillain. And said in the scariest, deepest, most hypnotizing voice, "I don't give a damn what you think about me, but if you speak while I am speaking again, we are going to have a problem."

I immediately imagined what Dad would have said about Mr. Thibodo if he'd been there.

I pictured Dad with his coffee, leaning back in one of those creaky theater chairs saying,

If you can somehow do a deep, booming voice that brings silence immediately, do it. That is a gift.

Rock climbing was not something Dad would have ever done, but I guess that's why it was fun to do with Grandpa.

Dad would have said something like, *Why climb a fake mountain?*

And I guess he would have been right, but I liked doing it anyway.

I liked the way Grandpa's face always twitched a little whenever Blaine tried to correct him on something. Grandpa HATES being told what to do.

And I liked the way Grandpa could tell this made me laugh so he laughed about it too.

It's cool when you learn how people work. Like the things that make them happy or sad. And the stuff that gets under their skin. I didn't really know all that stuff about Grandpa before because every time we saw him it was on quick trips with Dad. And Dad kinda takes all the attention anywhere he goes. But now I know way more about Grandpa.

Like how he hates it when Blaine calls him Big Guy, which Blaine does about every thirty seconds.

My face hurts from laughing so much.

"C'mon, Big Guy, grab the yellow rock this time. Purple is for beginners. You're ready for the yellow rock!"

Blaine was wearing a shirt that said "You rock my world." I could tell Grandpa hated that too.

But for some reason, Grandpa didn't complain, even though I could tell he definitely wanted to.

"Hey, Walter!"

I looked down.

Jamal from school was waving from the ground next to a guy who looked like a fatter, balder version of him. Like a Jamal from the future.

"Hey!" I yelled down.

When Grandpa raised his eyebrow at me, I said, "Jamal goes to school with me."

He and his dad started climbing on the blue rocks next to us. Blue is advanced.

"Hey!" Jamal said when he got up. He climbed up pretty quickly.

"Hey," I said. "This is my grandpa."

Grandpa nodded at him and then nodded at Jamal's dad, who was out of breath.

"Dad, this is the guy who does the voices for the morning announcements."

Grandpa kinda tilted his head to listen, and I realized I'd never really told him about that.

"Oh, yeah?" said Jamal's dad. "I've heard a lot about you. You do Kermit?"

"Do it for him," said Jamal, when he got up close enough to elbow me.

I rolled my eyes.

"C'mon," he said.

So I did it.

First the Kermit voice.

Followed by the Queen.

And then the alien voice from my first day.

Jamal laughed. His dad whistled. And Grandpa looked impressed. Even Blaine, who had paused his motivational speech about facing your fears, clapped.

"Alright, we're heading up," said Jamal. "I'm going over that one today," he said. It was this huge piece of the wall that stuck out at a weird angle that until that moment I thought was only for display because it looked too hard to actually climb.

"I'll be right behind you," his dad groaned. "Way

behind you. Nice meeting you guys."

Grandpa and I jumped down off the wall and started undoing our harnesses.

"I guess that art school is working out," he said.

"Yeah, Dad would have liked it," I said. Then I stopped and realized that made it sound like Dad wasn't coming back from wherever he'd gone.

"He'll see it," said Grandpa.

Even though him saying that made me feel good, I could tell it didn't really make Grandpa feel good.

"See you guys next week," Blaine said.

When he walked out to the parking lot, Grandpa looked over at me and said, "You're really good at voices. Like your dad."

It makes me feel good whenever someone says I'm like Dad.

"I want a goose to lay golden eggs for Easter," Fil shouted in a whiny voice.

After rock climbing, she'd come over to practice our lines together. Then I practiced the lines at the end when Wonka and Charlie become friends, and Fil said, "That was really good. But every time you've practiced that scene with Buttcream, it has SUCKED. You gotta pretend he's someone else."

I knew she was right.

Grandpa made beef stew with peas and carrots for dinner, and we practiced lines the whole way through the meal, and Grandpa even laughed a few times, which made everything seem a thousand times better. Normal even.

Probably how things are supposed to be with a schedule and a bedtime. Like families on TV.

"Can you do Darth Vader?" Fil asked when we were clearing our plates.

I cleared my throat and put my hand over my mouth to make a weird rasping noise.

Apple Grove Performing Arts Academy,
rasp *rasp*
Today's lunch specials are *rasp*
Dino chicken nuggets
And macaroni and cheese.
Please remind your parents that the pickup line after school must move quickly *rasp* and that no one *rasp* not even the Sith Lord *rasp* can park in the loading zone. *rasp*

Should you ignore these warnings * rasp*
I am ready to welcome you to the dark side. *rasp*

Fil laughed a lot, and Grandpa said from the other room, "Now, that one was perfect."
Darth Vader, I thought. *Check.*

TEN

TECHNICALLY JAMAL IS IN the acting conservatory with me, but he takes tons of the dance classes too.

"It's awesome," Jamal said. "My dad says it's like learning how to breathe music."

"Does he dance?" I asked while we were lining up outside the auditorium.

"Really badly." Jamal laughed.

I'm not sure I would have ever called what Jamal does at dance class "dancing." It looked to me like mostly they just moved like their arms and legs like they weren't attached to their bodies.

So when Mr. Thibodo told us we were all going to watch the new dance for the third Oompa Loompa song when Violet Beauregarde turns into a blueberry, I was expecting it to be some break-dance thing like I'd already seen Jamal do during other rehearsals.

But then Mr. Thibodo explained that he liked to take bits and pieces from other Broadway shows to get us used to different styles.

I didn't know what that meant, and a few people started whispering about some show that was pretty famous.

"What's *STOMP*?" I asked Fil.

She shrugged, but Jamal overheard and said, "You'll see. It's amazing."

Jamal and Pete came out onstage holding—

"Are those trash can lids?" Fil whispered.

Mr. Thibodo shushed her, but they were definitely blue trash can lids. Right after Violet's blueberry scenes, the Oompa Loompas raced across the stage dancing on them, beating the ground with lids on their hands and feet in a single rhythm.

Then the house lights went out, and a few people screamed as a whole bunch of blue twinkle lights lit up the stage around the dancers while they stomped. The lights bounced onto the stage like drops of—

". . . Blueberry juice," Fil whispered.

It was really cool, but also super gross to think about them squashing the juice out of a giant blueberry girl. In the movie, they just sort of rolled her away, but this made it seem much more . . . I dunno . . . creepy? Like they were stomping around in her blueberry blood.

The dancing was amazing, though.

All plays have costumes. But this is Apple Grove, so we have **COSTUMES** (insert jazz hands).

Mr. Thibodo had the high school fashion design students come in to take measurements and show us their sketches for our costumes. My designer's name was Li. He's a tall, skinny Chinese guy with a blue spike through his ear. He was wearing a really nice suit, which at first, I thought was weird, but Fil says all the Apple Grove High kids take all of their off-campus assignments seriously. Their designs go in their portfolio, which they need to apply to college art and design school.

They already do a lot of design work for their classes. Really cool stuff. Like, for their fashion show last year, Fil said, their theme was Living Earth, and they made these complicated costumes out of real flowers and vines and stuff. The pictures she had of it were super cool. Like what I think plants would be like if they came to life and walked around in heels.

They also had makeup design people come too, with stuff that had been donated by movie studios, so it all looked really professional.

Which made me a little nervous.

It was weird thinking that I have such an important role for a production where so many people are involved. It's a little bit like that children's book where three guys make soup by throwing a bunch of stuff in it. They call it stone soup, even though it's all the other stuff that makes it a soup.

"Did you always want to design clothes?" I asked Li. He was wearing a tiny bit of electric blue eye liner that I wouldn't have even noticed if it hadn't perfectly matched the fabric square in his suit pocket. He adjusted the collar of my jacket with a really serious expression, a little bit like a spy trying to defuse a bomb. And I guess I asked him because it was really quiet in the room and that always makes me uncomfortable. I think that's something I got from Dad.

I am always tempted to run my fingers across the chalkboard. I hate silence.

I didn't understand what that meant, because all of our classroom boards have dry erase markers, until I saw a movie where a guy did it and the screechy, awful noise made my skin tingle.

So anyway, for reasons unknown, I felt the need to keep talking while Li adjusted my wardrobe and Mr. Thibodo nodded approvingly in my direction.

"Yeah, I always wanted to design clothes," Li said. "It's what I'm supposed to do."

"How do you know what you're supposed to do?" I asked him.

Which is a pretty personal question. Like, I don't even know Li, and I doubted he really wanted to get into a discussion with a kid in fifth grade, but the question jumped out before I could push it back down.

Luckily, Li didn't seem to think it was too personal. Or if he did, he didn't show it. He answered pretty quickly.

"I know because I feel most like myself while I'm creating with clothes. Everything else feels like work. This feels like me being me."

I stood there draped in fabric, absorbing the awesomeness of his words because no one had ever talked like that about growing up before.

I know I could've been cool and just left it there, but Li was just so confident. I couldn't help asking him more questions.

"But what about people who get stuck doing stuff they hate—just to, like, make a living?"

Then Li looked at me and said, "Nobody is stuck. They just think they're stuck."

Whoa, I thought. *What do you say when you've just had your mind blown?*

He finished pinning my sleeves and stood back to look at the fabric.

"It was a big deal to get chosen to do your costume. Lots of people wanted to do it. We kinda had to have a contest to see who got the gig."

"What kind of contest?" I asked.

"We needed to submit ideas and then people voted on them on Instagram," he said. Li handed me a drawing of what looked like me as Willy Wonka. "My boyfriend made the suggestion to take off the heels because he thought it would be too much, but you get the idea."

The drawing looked a little bit like how Willy Wonka looked in the old movie, but there was also something kinda cool and creepy about it too. Like Li had tried to combine *The Nightmare Before Christmas* and the Candyland board game into one costume. The suit was tight, and the shoes were pointy and seemingly designed to make me look taller and skinnier than I was. The top hat was my favorite part.

But not everyone was excited about what their designers had come up with. I could hear Travis arguing with his designer about her sketches. She had really curly blond hair, and when I turned around, she looked like she was trying not to cry.

"This is boring! Completely uninspired," Travis whined. "And it looks like rags!"

"Charlie Bucket is poor," she was trying to explain while also trying to catch Mr. Thibodo's eye from across the room, but then I couldn't hear her anymore over the sound of Pete and Jamal laughing at the look on Travis's face. He looked like he'd just gotten underwear for Christmas.

Earlier today, Blaine gave Grandpa a boost to the first rock on the harder course by touching his butt. Watching him, you would have thought Grandpa had been electrocuted. He definitely climbed faster, though. We'd managed to make it all the way to the top of the more difficult path, and when we pulled ourselves over the ledge and looked around for a bit, Grandpa said, "Jump down?"

And I said, "Sure. Blaine will catch you."

Then I laughed at the sour look on Grandpa's face.

Sometimes when Dad calls, everything feels normal. Like tonight.

We did voices together.

"C'mon, you're not even trying!" he said over the phone.

"You be Bert," I said.

"No way. I'm totally Ernie." He laughed.

I gave in and did Bert's voice. He was Ernie. We nailed it.

Actually, I think *Sesame Street* is where I learned I could do this. Where I learned I could make myself sound like other people, and there's still something kinda amazing about how much Dad still gets into it. Our Snuffy and Big Bird are great, too, but there's more magic in our Bert and Ernie.

"So, I hear you're killing it at school with your voices?"

Grandpa must have mentioned the morning announcements again.

"Yeah, I guess," I said. "People have been able to guess all of them right so far."

Dad paused and then said in a serious voice, "Maybe that's 'cause you're doing famous people. No challenge there. Try doing a regular guy."

"A regular guy?" I asked.

"Yes, a regular guy. Not some artsy-fartsy celebrity," he said, in a perfect imitation of Grandpa.

There were a full five minutes where we didn't say anything. We just laughed, and the sound filled the whole room. It probably filled Dad's room too. Wherever he was.

It felt so good I didn't want to ruin it by asking when he was coming home to get me. I didn't mention it. I just let the laughs die out, like when you let the fizz out of a soda.

ELEVEN

SCHOOL HAD JUST ENDED for the day. Jamal, Pete, Fil, and I were practicing our entrance for the first scene of the play out in the quad before rehearsal started when something weird happened with Fil.

I didn't even know what was going on until Peter and Jamal suddenly looked like they'd both forgotten how to speak.

"Hey, look at Filomena," Rachel said.

Because of course she happened to be there at the exact moment that something awkward happened to Fil.

Rachel was always looking for a way to embarrass Fil, and Fil's goal in life was to not be embarrassed by anyone. Ever. But in this case, I could see why Fil was looking down at her crotch in horror as a red stain blossomed there.

Even though somewhere in my head I knew what was happening, I didn't know what to do. I sort of moved toward Fil in slow motion while Rachel and her friends evil-laughed together. I had no real plan. I just knew that I needed to put myself between her and Rachel—even if I wasn't exactly sure what I was defending her against. Somewhere at the back of my thoughts, I knew I had a sweatshirt I could give her.

Rachel was standing there with a smirk on her face, like she was seizing this opportunity to be awful.

Which is weird, because guys are mean too, but we're mean differently. Guys will throw a punch at you. They might laugh in your face and do something to embarrass you, but girls are different. They want everyone to see it when they embarrass you. They want everyone to be a part of the experience to make that person feel as small as possible.

The laughter kicked up again.

Then out of nowhere, when it looked like Fil might crumble into a pile of broken Fil pieces, Sarabeth appeared.

"Hey," she said to Rachel.

Rachel looked up at her in shock because I think she thought Sarabeth was a teacher for a second.

"Aren't you the girl who slept with her head on a cat turd at her own slumber party?"

One of the other girls laughed, and Rachel turned red.

"How about you disappear and take the smell with you?"

Rachel stormed off, and Sarabeth very quickly took off her sweatshirt and wrapped it tightly around Fil's waist like I should have done immediately.

"Do you have a pad or a tampon?" Sarabeth asked. Fil shook her head.

"Okay, c'mon," she said. Then Sarabeth looked at me like she'd just remembered I was there and said, "Tell Mr. Thibodo she'll be late."

And she pushed Fil off to the bathroom, and I stood there trying to figure things out.

Jamal shook me out of my stupor when he thought to finally ask, "Where did she come from?" Which was a fair question, because her school was across the street.

Was she, like, some kind of superhero?

When Fil came back into rehearsal, Sarabeth was sitting in the back of the theater with her earphones on doing homework.

"She was fast," I whispered to Fil when I caught up to her onstage. Then I blushed and stared down at my feet. "Look, I'm sorry I didn't—I didn't know what to do." I sort of trailed off, and luckily, she laughed.

"It's a period, Wally. You can't really help me with that."

She smiled, and I felt my face get hot again.

"Also," she said, "that's why I was out sick the other day. Mom says she had cramps like this too before she got her period. Luckily, I can take some stuff that helps."

I nodded but had no idea what she was talking about.

"Mom told Sarabeth to walk over here after school so she could pick both of us up for a dentist appointment," Fil said. "Most rehearsal days, she catches a ride home with a friend."

Normally, Fil would have also said something about the way Sarabeth was pretending the whole play was beneath her even though she was only, like, a year and a half older, but not today.

I looked out at the audience where Sarabeth was sitting. She was ignoring all the other kids flitting about, but she was also, even from the back row of the auditorium, still watching over Fil, ready to stomp on Rachel's (or anyone else's) face if she needed to.

Sisters can be weirdly vicious to each other, but also weirdly protective of each other. Seems like it might almost be worth it to have one.

I was glad Sarabeth was around to handle the situation, but I also decided that next time I was at the drugstore with Grandpa I'd get something for Fil in case she needs it again. I think that's pretty much all I can do.

That said, explaining to Grandpa why I needed a tampon or a menstrual pad in my backpack was going to be interesting.

The next day, Fil played tetherball with me and Jamal and Sam and William. After recess we had computer lab, but when we got there, we had a sub. It was Mrs. Butte from the front desk. When I walked in, she wrinkled her nose, which made her look even more raisiny than usual.

"Mr. Chu's wife just went into labor, and your actual sub is running late," she said. "You can all do your typing program quietly while you wait."

No one did this.

We just started talking. Quietly at first, then louder.

"Saw you at Donut Holes on Sunday," said Pete. "That old dude your grandpa?"

"Yeah," I said.

"He comes to get you to take you out for donuts?" he asked.

"Well, I live with him now, so—"

"Why?" asked Jamal.

"That's not really any of your business," said Fil.

"It's okay," I whispered. Then she did that thing to Jamal where you try to get someone to stop talking because you know the next thing they're going to say might ruin everything.

"My dad is traveling for work, and he couldn't take me with him."

"Is that what he told you?" said Travis.

He was leaning back in one of the two computer chairs that spin. His hair was all plastered to his face and super sweaty from recess, because he's one of those kids that starts sweating the minute he throws a ball.

"Yeah," I said. "He couldn't take me with him."

"Well, that part is true."

The room was suddenly very quiet. Mrs. Butte was standing at the open classroom door on the ramp, tapping her foot while she waited for the sub. She clearly couldn't hear what the class was doing.

Travis turned his computer screen to me, where I saw a headline from a local online magazine that read "Local Legend Edward Ellis Admitted to Rehab." Then there was an old video of Dad falling off a stage. I knew it was an old video because he threw that shirt out a long time ago. I watched him fall like it was happening in slow motion. He stumbled up and then fell backward again.

It was like I was falling with him.

"Guess you didn't know your dad is a drunk," Travis said.

I've never hit anyone before. I'd thought about it, sure, but I'd never actually done it.

And even though I wanted to hit Travis, I didn't.

I shoved Travis to the ground. Fil stood up, but she wasn't quick enough to stop me. The commotion caught Mrs. Butte's attention.

"You boys knock it off! I do not get paid enough for this!" she screamed.

But we weren't listening to her. We were rolling on the floor trying to fight without really knowing how. I held on to the front of Travis's shirt, and we crashed into the computer chairs until Mrs. Butte dumped the water from the vase on Mr. Chu's desk on us.

The water smelled bad and was slimy and had little flecks of brown stuff in it because there had been half dead plants sitting in it for a while.

But it worked, I guess, because we stopped fighting, and the substitute teacher walked in just in time to see Mrs. Butte marching me and Travis out of the room.

TWELVE

MRS. PUDUMJEE MET WITH us in her office, but not together. Travis walked in first and looked back at me like he'd just won something.

"Close the door, please," she said.

So he closed the door, and I sat in the chair out in the waiting area like I had on the first day of school.

Your dad is a drunk.

Those were the only words I heard in my head.

I was mad because I didn't know.

I was with him all the time, and I didn't know.

How could I not know?

But I was also mad because when other people look at that article about Dad, "drunk" is the only word they're going to see. When they see that video of him, it's the only word that they'll hear.

Drunk.

They won't see "funny." They won't see "happy." They won't see "smart."

They'll just see "drunk."

It's one of those words that eats all the other words up.

Mrs. Butte kept looking at me and shaking her head, and it made me really not sorry I kept calling her Raisin Face in my head.

Travis's mom walked into the front office wearing big sunglasses. She took them off and looked at me for, like, half a second before pulling out her phone and tapping something into it angrily before sitting down in a chair opposite me.

Mrs. Pudumjee opened the door a minute later, and Travis's mom went in.

Five minutes later, Travis's mom had her arm around Travis, who was crying dramatically.

"Walter," said Mrs. Pudumjee.

I walked in and looked around. The office was the same, but for some reason, Wonder Woman in the poster on the wall looked a bit more judgmental.

"Have a seat," she said. "I already filled your grandpa in. He's on his way."

Mrs. Pudumjee didn't seem happy or fun today. She seemed tired.

"I didn't mean to shove him," I said. "I'm sorry."

I looked down at my feet.

"The article made you angry," she said.

I nodded.

"Can you tell me why?"

I shook my head.

I was determined not to cry in her office, but I could feel it building up, hot behind my eyes.

"Is it because you didn't want other people to know?" she asked gently.

"*I* didn't know," I said. "Not really, anyway."

"Was it what Travis called him that bothered you?"

I nodded.

"Because that's all they know," I explained.

She nodded, and I think she understood. She wasn't just pretending to understand like most adults. She knew I wasn't trying to be a jerk.

"Go home for the rest of the day, and we'll see you on Monday." She smiled, and I tried to smile back, but my mouth wouldn't move.

"That's it?" I asked.

"Well, yeah. That's a one-day suspension for fighting. Don't do it again," she said seriously. "I have a visual arts presentation to get to, but you can wait for your grandpa in the front office."

I put my hand on the door handle and pushed it open.

"Oh, and Walter," Mrs. Pudumjee said. "I can't wait for the play. I've never seen Mr. Thibodo so excited."

I tried to smile, but my lips didn't seem to bend that way today.

I stepped into the front office, and my brain wound everything down to slow motion. The weird thing was I could have searched Dad's name at any time. I could have read it myself if I'd looked for it, but I hadn't. I just believed Dad when he told me he needed to go away to do something and that I couldn't come with him.

He'd never lied to me before. At least I thought he hadn't.

The more I thought about it, the more it made sense that Dad had a problem.

The bottles. There were always bottles around. Never out in the open for people to see, but I always heard them clinking whenever he took the garbage out. I think one of the strangest things that shouldn't really be strange about living at Grandpa's was how quiet he was when he took out the trash.

Dad always had a drink, even though I knew he wasn't thirsty. And he always had a bottle of something that he poured into whatever regular drink he had when he thought I wasn't looking. Like his coffee or his orange juice.

He'd joke about it, too. Something about it being five o'clock somewhere. But I don't really understand what that means.

Sometimes he took really long naps in weird places. Like on the floor of his bedroom with his head leaning against his laundry basket.

And sometimes when I got home from school, he'd fill a short glass with amber liquid, and he'd say something like, *I just need to relax for a bit. Then let's go do something fun.* Then he'd smile, finish his drink, and we'd walk out the door and we *would* do something fun.

I thought about the article again.

Edward Ellis Admitted to Rehab.

There was some information about *Hometown*

Tunes, his old bands, some of the cover songs he'd done recently, and about a scholarship he'd gotten in high school. And there was even a link to his YouTube channel that I'd stopped listening to when I started living with Grandpa.

I looked around and decided I wasn't going to wait here for Grandpa. I was not going to sit here while Raisin Face stared at me and the other teachers walked by feeling sorry for me. Or for Fil to come by and try to make me feel better. Nope.

So where are we going? Dad would have asked.

I imagined him standing there with his Converse shoes and a cup of coffee in one hand and his guitar case in the other.

We *aren't going anywhere*, I would have told him.

You *lied to me*, I would have said.

I imagined the way his face would fall and the hurt behind his eyes.

That's when I noticed the blue button that I pushed months ago when I first started doing the announcements, back when everyone thought I was just a kid who was really good at voices. Not some kid who didn't know the truth about his dad.

Raisin Face got up from her chair, straightened

her bubble gum pink sweater, and tucked a folder under her arm before disappearing into the copy room down the hall. Mrs. Pudumjee wouldn't be back in the office for a while.

The blue button stared at me again.

It had the same pull as it did before. Like it was Earth and I was a big fat comet heading straight for it.

All I could think of was how good it would feel to be someone else for a second.

So I moved quickly and pushed the button, and a voice came out.

But it wasn't the Queen. Or Darth Vader. Or Big Bird. Or Wonka.

It was Dad.

Hey, Apple Grove Performing Arts—
This isn't your regularly scheduled announcement.
I'm not supposed to be talking right now, and I'm sorry I'm probably interrupting a lesson for some math you'll never use, but here's something you should know—
Adults are not perfect.
We mess up too.

Sometimes we suck.

And sometimes it's more important to remember that people are mostly doing their best.

Maybe that's all we can ask.

I clicked the blue button again. It was time to get out, because I could hear Raisin Face running toward the mic she'd left unattended.

Luckily, the teacher's lounge was empty, so it was easy to race straight through it and out the back door. Then I hopped the kindergarten fence on the other side of the parking lot. I mean, I was in trouble and being sent home anyway, so why not take off running?

Running normally really sucks. It was my least favorite part of PE, because it's pointless. Like hamsters on a wheel. But if you're trying to get away from something, then it works wonders.

People who like running will also probably tell you that it gives you a chance to think.

That's annoyingly true because while I was running, I thought about what it would have been like if Dad had really made that announcement. He would have shrugged, maybe leaned back in his chair.

Maybe even winked at Raisin Face when she returned to her desk.

The announcement was something he'd said before. Maybe not exactly, and maybe it hadn't made it into the journal, but he'd definitely said something like it before.

No one would know it was Dad's voice, but that didn't matter either. I wasn't doing it for them. *They* weren't the ones who needed to hear him.

I wanted to be somewhere else as fast as possible, but I didn't want to go home.

So my feet took me to Donut Holes, where I sat and waited for the familiar sound of footsteps that I knew were coming.

Grandpa didn't walk over to my table right away. He went to the counter and asked Louise for his usual donut and coffee and then scanned the top row and pointed to a chocolate long John with Bavarian cream. Before he sat down, he grabbed one of the glass bottles of milk Louise keeps in a mini fridge next to the register. The old-fashioned kind with the cream that floats to the top, which sounds gross but is actually really good.

"You're a lot of work today," he said, setting the

drinks on the table first.

"I didn't want to wait for you," I told him.

"Yeah. I figured."

"You're not mad?"

"It wasn't hard to figure out where you might end up," Grandpa said, lowering himself into the chair. "But I'd be lying if I told you I wasn't a little pissed."

He slid the donut bag over the table.

"It's not Sunday, though," I said, reaching for it.

"Guess we're all having a strange day, then."

I took a bite of what was probably the best donut of my life and looked up at Grandpa, who was watching me cautiously.

"So, he hasn't been working," I said finally.

Grandpa shook his head.

"So, he lied to me."

Grandpa shook his head again.

"He said he couldn't take you with him. That part was true. But he never actually said he was working," Grandpa said.

"That. Is. Bullshit," I said, shoving the rest of the donut into my mouth.

Grandpa looked a little shocked, but he laughed.

"You're right," he said, leaning back.

"Is he okay?" I asked.

"He's okay," Grandpa said.

"I mean, is he better now?" I asked.

"It doesn't work like that," Grandpa said. And his voice sounded tired all of a sudden. For some reason, that made me sad.

"How does it work?" I asked.

"Look I'm not an expert," Grandpa said. "But it's not something that ever goes away. It'll always be there. And I don't expect you to really understand, because it's complicated, but—"

"Is he a drunk?" I whispered.

Even though the place was empty except for Louise, saying it out loud made it feel worse. I knew it wasn't just me because Grandpa winced like I'd shouted it.

"Your dad is a lot of things," he said. "And sometimes you love a person, but you don't love everything about them. Sometimes it's better that way. No one is perfect. We're people."

I was still angry because I didn't know anything, and it feels like the worst kind of lie when someone doesn't tell you something on purpose. Like they're hiding it because they don't trust you or because you're not old enough to handle it or something stupid like that. But even though I was mad, my brain was still searching for the one true thing. The thing I was feeling most.

"I miss Dad," I said. My eyes hurt. It was the first time I'd said that out loud. But I did. I missed him, a lot, and I just wanted to say it out loud.

I didn't want to cry, but once it gets all hot behind your eyes, you can't really hold it off forever. You can't help it. Grandpa did something he'd never done before. He slid across the little bench to where I was sitting and sat down next to me. Then he put his arm around me and squeezed.

We sat like that for a long time.

"You know, I actually thought I was hearing your dad when I got to school."

I turned to stare up at him.

"You were there when I did that announcement?"

"Yeah," he said. "There are speakers outside. When I got out of my car, I heard you, and I thought it was your dad." He took a sip of his coffee and said, "Damn, you're good."

"So, am I in trouble for that too?"

"I think you get a pass since you were already

in trouble for fighting in school. Funny how that worked out."

"Oh. Am I in trouble for fighting?"

Grandpa knew I didn't mean with school, since school already sent me home. He knew I meant *am I in trouble at home because I was fighting at school?*

"Getting angry and taking a swipe at someone is generally not a good idea," Grandpa said seriously. "Unless you're defending yourself."

I looked down at the ground.

"But," he said, "it sounds like that little turd had it coming. Just try not to do it again, okay?"

I smiled.

I knew that was definitely not a perfect answer, but it had been a weird day, so it worked.

THIRTEEN

BY THE TIME WE got home, I wanted more than anything to slip into someone else's head. I didn't want to have to think about anything anymore.

"I'll be downstairs if you want to talk some more," Grandpa said. He didn't sit in his chair or go into the kitchen or even hang up his keys. He sorta just waited for me to head up the stairs and close the door.

Not even Tiberius followed me this time.

I went into my bathroom and stood on the little step stool that I use to get the toilet paper off the top shelf and just looked in the mirror.

For a second, I pretended that Dad was looking back at me. He didn't say anything. He just smiled. Then he took a long drink and set the glass down, and I realized I didn't want to talk to him right now, even if he was just an imagined person temporarily living in my mirror.

I opened the medicine cabinet and pulled out my floss.

I always floss when I'm mad at Sarabeth, and I can't get away with tackling her, Fil once told me.

That's weird, I said.

Yeah, she agreed. *But my grandma told me it's better to do something good when you're angry so you don't regret it later. So I floss because how can you regret flossing? Plus Sarabeth has had, like, four cavities, and I'm never going to let that happen to my teeth. So I floss when I'm mad.*

So I flossed.

I was still mad when I closed the medicine cabinet. But at least imaginary Dad wasn't in the mirror anymore.

But that didn't stop me from thinking about the last time I saw him or the day he dropped me off.

There's not a lot to tell about our trip across the country to Grandpa's house. I mean, sure, there were lots of stops at McDonald's, but I guess there is one night I remember pretty well.

It was a day before Dad said we had to leave, and

it was one of those gigs that I was allowed to go to.

I brought my homework to one of the booths, near the back of the place he was playing, and propped my math book against the ketchup and mustard caddy at the end of the table. The waitress brought me chicken fingers and chocolate milk, and I pretended to do my homework while Dad played.

It had been a good night.

Dad had been invited to this new restaurant that just opened. The owner was a big fan of his performances on *Hometown Tunes*, and tons of people were crowding into the place. At least I didn't have to fight the crowds. I had my own spot to watch the show. So it was cool. It was one of those times when I could tell how much my dad loves music. I could see how he lets it kinda flow out of him.

There were lots of people walking over to him to put tips in the jar. Some of them bought him drinks.

I never liked that. I didn't like when they bought him drinks and tried talking to him, because he always sat and drank with them. He always gave them his time. And all those people were just being nice because it's something you do when someone plays a song you like, but I always kinda wanted my dad to say no. At least once. Because I knew he wasn't thirsty, and I just wanted him to come over and sit with me. His kid. Not some random strangers.

Anyway, it was a good night for Dad.

Lots of people came in to listen to him sing. Even the owner was happy. I could tell because he walked over to clap my dad on the back. At the end of his set, Dad even played his version of "Pure Imagination" from the *Willy Wonka and the Chocolate Factory* movie. He did it the way I love—Fast. Slow. Fast. Fast. Slow.

We were there late. Way later than I was used to being out, even though I'd never really had a bedtime. I wound up falling asleep at the table.

I'm too big to be carried, but Dad picked me up anyway, and I did that thing that I used to do when I was small where I pretended that I was still asleep after he picked me up so I didn't have to walk. It wasn't something I always got away with, but that night Dad was in the mood to believe me.

He carried me out to the car and buckled me in, and I could tell the parking lot was empty. He fumbled with his keys, but he got the car going after struggling to find the ignition for a sec.

Then we took off, and I fell asleep for real.

For a few minutes at least.

Until Dad slammed his feet on the brakes.

And I woke up pretty fast when the car spun around as I started to scream. The traffic lights all blended together in a red and green streak of light, and I looked over at Dad who looked scared for the first time that I'd ever seen.

His knuckles were white on the wheel, and he had his fingers wrapped around it like the car was a rodeo horse and he was trying to keep it from bucking us out the windows.

Then the car finally stopped.

"Walter, are you okay?"

"I think so," I told him.

He reached over and put his hand on my chest, then on my face to make sure.

There'd been a curve in the road, and we'd hit the corner of a sign with our front bumper. That's why we'd spun around. It was an empty road, so nobody was around.

"Dad, I'm okay," I said again.

He nodded, but he didn't say anything, and he didn't let go of my shoulder.

I'm not sure how long it took us to get home. Way longer than it should have, but when we finally got back to the apartment, Dad sat with me until I fell asleep, but he didn't play his guitar. That was weird because he always played at night before bed, no matter how late it was. It always helped me sleep, and he said it helped him untangle all the stuff in his head even though he never told me what that stuff was.

I remember a lot of things about that night, and I try to focus on the good stuff but I remember all the stuff that wasn't so good too.

I remember that Dad called Grandpa.

I remember that even though he'd said we'd never move back to his hometown, he packed up a bunch of our stuff in the boxes we hadn't even finished unpacking from our last move.

And I remember that he cried.

And it's not like Dad hadn't cried before. We'd watched sad movies together, and once I saw him smash a hammer directly into his thumb, which led to a lot of swearing and crying, but this time I *heard* him cry and it felt wrong.

Because it wasn't like him.

Dad was happy. He was always excited about something. He told me I could do anything and that he would always be proud of me and that the world was a better place because I was in it. Happy stuff.

I never realized that people who are sad sometimes try to make the happy stuff louder than it is.

The next day I helped him finish packing, and that's when we left for Grandpa's house.

"Walter," Grandpa called up from downstairs. "Fil's here." Only he didn't really raise his voice. It was quiet in the house, so I could hear everything that was going on downstairs without even having to open my door.

"Okay," I said. I was sitting on the floor of my bedroom, leaning against the wall.

"Hey," said Fil. "Can I come in?" Tiberius waddled in after her.

She sat on the floor next to Tiberius for a bit. Tiberius doesn't really like her yet, and I could tell she was trying not to take that personally.

"You knew?" I asked her.

She nodded. Of course she knew. Fil probably googled my dad's name the minute I told her he was a musician. That article probably popped up months ago.

It was just me who didn't know anything.

"Do you want to talk?" she asked.

"Not really," I said.

"Okay," she said. She pulled a new pack of Starbursts out of her pocket and pulled out all the pinks and reds and put them in a little tower in front of me.

Then she did something she'd never done before. She kissed my cheek before heading downstairs.

It wasn't like that, though. Really.

I don't think it was a *kiss* kiss.

It was just Fil being Fil.

I think.

And sure, it felt nice, but I just wanted to keep being mad for a while.

She understood that.

Dad used to say if you're mad at someone, it's a good idea to make a list of all the stuff you like about them.

Like he knew I'd be mad at him someday and that I would need that advice.

And I really wanted to, but I think maybe I was too angry to write down good stuff about Dad.

I didn't even want to look at the orange journal.

I wanted to know why he didn't tell me. I wanted to know if he was lying about anything else.

"Your dad is on the phone," Grandpa said through the door.

"I don't want to talk to him," I said.

The words felt hot and sticky when they came out, and I knew that when I went to the mirror to wash my face, I'd be picturing Dad standing there too.

Can we do Bert and Ernie? he would ask. *Or you be Luke and I'll be Vader?*

That's how it would have gone.

I know Grandpa stood there on the other side of the door for a while, because I didn't hear the footsteps right away, but he didn't say anything else.

I fell asleep before dinner, and he didn't wake me up.

Until the next morning, when he pulled the sheets off my bed and yelled, "RISE AND SHINE! IT'S A BEAUTIFUL MOOOOORNING!"

And I wanted to evaporate into the floorboards.

FOURTEEN

"GOOOOOOOD MORNING!" GRANDPA BELLOWED again.

It's times like these that I remember that he was in the marines.

"Up," Grandpa said, standing over my bed. He was dressed in his workout clothes.

"Not a school day," I said, rubbing my eyes.

"Up," he said again. "We're going to the gym. Get dressed."

"Again?" I asked. "We were just there, like, yesterday."

Maybe the day before yesterday? I wasn't sure. I just wanted to sleep.

He sounded serious, and I really didn't want to get up, but I didn't want Grandpa to come back into the room and do that clapping thing he does when I don't get up right away.

He handed me a banana on my way down the stairs, and Tiberius didn't even bother moving when we left the house.

I ate the banana and watched Grandpa drive. I had to blink a few times when I saw the gym swarming with people.

"Why is it so crowded?" I asked.

They were wearing different colored T-shirts with team names and everything.

RACE TO THE TOP COMPETITION

I'd completely forgotten about this, because I never in a million years thought Grandpa would want to enter. This was for serious climbers. People who practiced every day. I stared at him.

"Ready?" he asked.

"We're seriously doing this?"

"We're seriously doing this," he said.

"But we suck. Like, a lot. And it's not like we could be good if we tried hard. We actually suck, and there's no getting around that."

"Yeah," he said. "Get out of the car."

Blaine was there, and he almost dropped his

clipboard when he saw Grandpa and me, but c'mon, there was no way we'd suck more than *everyone* there.

But actually, we did.

Grandpa and I started off at the beginners climb, the one we'd climbed a couple days ago. We did fine there. Then we moved onto the intermediate wall that we practiced every week. I looked over at Grandpa, expecting something to be different, but nope.

We still sucked.

We both slipped a lot. I think Blaine felt sorry for me because he was lifting me a little from the ground. It probably looked like I was climbing the wall with my face.

Blaine yelled, "Reach for the blue rock, gentlemen!"

There was nobody there like us. Even Jamal and his dad hadn't shown up to this, and they were actually pretty good.

But Grandpa had this look in his eye. The kind of look he had when I wouldn't eat my vegetables that first time.

So we pulled ourselves up at a snail's pace, and after a while, I heard someone shout.

KEEP GOING, WALLY!

I looked down, and Fil was sitting next to Sarabeth on the bleachers the gym set up for the competition. Fil was holding up a sign that read

WE'RE HERE TO CATCH YOU!

Then Sarabeth held up a sign that said

PLEASE DON'T SQUISH US

I laughed. What was kinda funny was that this isn't something that Sarabeth would normally go to. And she definitely would not have gone with Fil. It would have been way too embarrassing. But they were sitting together like it was something they did all the time.

"You told Fil?" I asked Grandpa while he clutched one of the fat yellow beginner's rocks.

"I told her mom," he said. "Figured we'd need encouragement to finish."

It was at that moment that Grandpa's hand slipped, and he swung away from the wall. Since I'd been watching him, I lost my balance too, and we both sort of hung in our harnesses there like sad kites tangled in a tree.

"I think you distracted me enough from Dad," I told him, trying to face him, but failing because I kept spinning away from him in my harness.

"You knew that's what I was doing?" he asked. I nodded.

We both hung there while Blaine shouted, *"Grab the blue rocks, gentlemen!"* from the ground. Fil took pictures with Sarabeth's phone.

"You want to call him?" Grandpa asked.

"No," I said.

"Are you—"

"I'm sure," I said.

He sighed.

"Well, let's figure out how to get down. I told Fil's mom I'd take you guys out for burgers if you want. You know. For opening night."

"Thanks," I said.

We eventually got back to solid ground and collected our free T-shirts.

Bright yellow ones we'd never wear.

Blaine told us how proud he was of our commitment, and Grandpa thanked him. And it wasn't a fake thank-you. It was Grandpa trying really hard to accept someone else's praise even though he probably felt he didn't deserve it.

Then Fil, Sarabeth, me, and Grandpa got burgers down the street at a place called Jeb's, where he used to take my dad.

"Are you ready for the play?" Sarabeth asked me. She'd hardly ever spoken to me directly, but I just nodded.

"Of course he's ready," said Fil. "He IS Wonka."

It wasn't super profound, but I appreciated it.

We dropped Fil and Sarabeth off at their house and drove back to find Tiberius waiting in the window for us. It was like he knew that we had messages on the answering machine.

FIFTEEN

ANSWERING MACHINE RECORDING:

"Walter, it's me.

Dad.

I just wanted to say break a leg tonight. I'm proud of you. I love you."

Then he called back and left another message.

"Walter, it's me again. Dad. That's not all I wanted to say. I wanted to say I'm sorry.

I wanted to say I miss being in the same house with you. I miss seeing you every day. I miss you so much it hurts.

But if I say those things to you when I call, and if I hear your voice for too long, then I want to come running back. And I want to be better when I come back.

Just know that I love you and that you can be mad at me. I deserve it.

I just hope that the minute I *can* hug you again, you won't hate me too much to let me.

Every good thing I am is because of you."

Then he hung up.

SIXTEEN

GRANDPA WAS BACKSTAGE WITH me, and I knew he was uncomfortable. I told him parents came into the cast room before the performance but he didn't have to because I knew he wasn't really into the drama stuff.

A boy in an Oompa Loompa costume was practicing his scales to our left. Grandpa avoided eye contact completely as if he was doing something totally embarrassing, like picking lint out of his belly button.

"You really don't have to hang out here," I told him. "You can go wait in your seat if you want."

He considered it for half a second, but there were a bunch of parents outside elbowing their way to the front so they could get a good spot for the pictures they weren't allowed to take.

"No, I'm okay," he said.

Then he was silent while I looked at myself in the

mirror finally fully dressed as Willy Wonka.

Dad would have said, "You're ready." And I pictured him holding a program and standing at the back of the theater because he couldn't sit still.

Travis was sitting a few feet from me. He was dressed in his Charlie costume, his expression was super serious—like he was reciting some acting thing in his head.

His mom lifted her gaze from her phone every few seconds to stare at me, but Grandpa was always ready for her. He looked back at her without blinking, just waiting for her to say something.

Then she'd finally look away or move to fix Travis's hair or tell him how great he was and that his butt cream commercial prepared him for greatness or something stupid like that.

"Walter, you ready?"

Mr. Thibodo didn't look nervous. He never looked nervous, but he also spoke a lot with his eyes. And his eyes were very clearly saying, *I know you're going through a lot and maybe feeling a lot, but please, please, please don't ruin my play.*

And I respected that.

"Yeah," I said. "I'm ready."

Fil says every one of Thibodo's plays has some sort of ritual that the actors do together to get ready, something that links them no matter where they go. Our ritual was singing the song "We Will Rock You" by Queen.

Which might not seem like a thing, but all I have to do is think about this song and I can pretty much see the entire cast dressed up and ready to rehearse. Fifty years from now, I could be buying prunes at the grocery store and this song might play and suddenly I won't be some old guy. I'll be exactly the age I am right now, dressed as Willy Wonka, waiting for the curtain to go up.

Grandpa was ready to go to his seat, but he was waiting until Travis's mom found hers before he left to sit down.

"I'm not leaving you alone with that woman," he'd said. "I'm not convinced she won't swallow you whole and spit out your bones."

"That's super gross," I said.

"Well, yeah. It would be," said Grandpa, handing me a greasy paper bag.

"For after," he said. I looked inside. It was a

frosted cinnamon bun in the shape of a heart.

"Yeah, sorry. Louise was trying something new, and I know you like to try different stuff. But you know, hearts . . ."

I hugged him.

"Thanks," I said.

"I'll go find my seat," Grandpa told me.

"Hey, you all set?" Jamal asked. I nodded. He was calm. He always looked like he was ready to be onstage. He started practicing his backflips with Peter as I watched Fil transform into Veruca Salt.

"You okay?" she asked.

"Why? Do I look nervous?" I asked her.

"No. You look normal. That's why I'm asking."

Her hair was straight, and she looked like she was dressed for a rich kid prep school.

"Let's do this," I said.

I know how performances work, but you have to admit, it's weird getting ready to do a pretend thing that you've practiced with a bunch of people. It's almost like everyone decides to have the same dream at exactly the same time.

And it's even weirder when other people come

watch you do the pretend thing that you've practiced. Like, what if they don't get it?

When I looked from behind the curtain, I could see Grandpa in the audience. I didn't think he'd see me, but he did. It was like he was looking at the spot he thought I might be, and he smiled and waved, and I waved back and then he put his hand up and mouthed something I didn't understand.

When I looked confused, he reached into his pocket and pulled out something the size of his fist.

"Why's your grandpa holding up a blue lump?" asked Fil.

I laughed, and he knew I got it. Then he tried to make Blaine's serious face, and even though he was a few rows away, I saw him perfectly and laughed again.

No idea where he got the blue rock from, but the message was clear.

Reach for the blue rock, gentlemen!

It wasn't *good luck* or *break a leg*, but Grandpa does his own thing.

When it was time for my big part, Li adjusted the sleeves of my costume, nodded approvingly, and I walked out onstage.

And I don't know how to explain it, but it was like breathing. I didn't even notice how quickly my lines flew out until we got to the song. A reprise at the end.

Dad's song. "Pure Imagination."

The one that always made me think of him, no matter what.

Now that I wanted to do anything but think of him, I couldn't imagine any song that was more annoying to sing. Especially since I knew they'd be doing it wrong.

Dad's version would be slower than—

I listened hard.

And paused.

As I listened, I realized that *this* intro *was* slower than it needed to be. It didn't sound the way it had during rehearsal. It sounded familiar in a way no one else would understand.

Slow. Then the repeated first line.

Just like how Dad sang it.

And I knew I must have been imagining it, but when I started singing the song, I sang it the way I would have if Dad had been there. It was something we'd practiced together. Something we'd watched when there was nothing else to watch. When we had been waiting for something. When we were avoiding something. Because it was the only movie we had for a long time, and sometimes you don't want to talk, you just want to listen and tune everything else out.

And even though everyone else looking at me would see an amazing costume and would hear me talking like Willy Wonka . . .

Anybody else who knew him would know that I was playing my dad.

Grandpa definitely knew.

Then the show was over and I heard the applause and the lights went out, and I could swear I heard the sound of Dad tapping the body of his guitar with his thumb, the way he always used to when he finished a song.

It made me think of something from the orange journal. Something I couldn't quite remember.

> It's a moment, Walter. Sometimes they're big, like winning something. Sometimes they're small, like just noticing something. And it's not always something you can explain. You just feel it.

It was like he was there.

* * *

We took our bows, and let me say this: applause is not overrated.

Yeah, it's weird to stand by yourself in the middle of a stage and have people make noise to show you that they like something you did.

But I like it.

I think it's something I'm always going to like.

And I know I've probably said it before, but it's cool that Apple Grove treats us like real artists.

Our stage is real.

Our costumes are like the ones they use in movies.

Even the backstage is set up like a real backstage with those bulb lights around the mirrors for the actors.

Mr. Thibodo clapped me on the shoulder when he got backstage, but he didn't say anything. Fil told me a while ago that he can barely talk on opening night, but a pat on the shoulder is always a good sign.

When she walked in, she hugged me.

"You were great," she said. "And Sarabeth said you were great too. I just saw her."

"You were the best Veruca," I told her.

"Better than the British girl in the movie?"

"Way better. Actually, she sucked big-time."

"I know," she said. "But it would be rude if I said it."

We both laughed.

Then Travis walked over, threw his hat on the back of my chair dramatically, and said:

"Walter, your performance showed real improvement, and we were lucky you went along with the new guitarist."

Fil was about to open her mouth. Probably to call him Butt Cream to his face, but I cut her off.

"Thanks, Travis."

New guitarist?

There was a steady hum of noise because everyone was excited. Jamal and Peter and the rest of the Oompa Loompas who had gotten covered in blue paint goo from the blueberry *STOMP* part were still soaking in the reaction to that scene. The whole audience had leaped to their feet when the trash can lids came out and Violet Beauregarde got the juice squeezed out of her.

"I'd never even heard of *STOMP*," said Peter, falling into a chair in front of his own mirror with lights. "But people like really love music with trash can lids."

"Amateurs," Travis said under his breath, shaking his head.

Eventually everyone started clearing out, but I still hadn't seen Grandpa yet. I just figured he was trying to make his way through the crowd.

After a few minutes, I was by myself in the room, packing up my stuff.

I heard footsteps behind me and just assumed it was Grandpa.

"I was wondering if I could get your autograph?"

I didn't turn around. I think it was because I didn't want to be disappointed. I just waited there, with my knees frozen to ground, holding the orange journal I was still trying to shove into my backpack on the floor.

"Mr. Thibodo let me step in last minute for that song," he said. "And I guess I just . . . Wow. You are so talented, Walter. I always knew you were, but wow . . . I just—"

I stood up, my back still to him and looked into the mirror. The lights from the giant bulbs illuminated him.

Dad in his Converse shoes.

Holding his guitar case.

Dad. Here. In real life.

And I wanted to be mad still because he'd lied. I really did. Nothing makes lying okay.

But I ran to him anyway, because that's what you do when hugging someone is the only thing that will fix what hurts.

And it felt good standing there with Dad. Neither of us saying anything. Just taking a deep breath to cry every so often, because how do you ever let go of someone you missed that much?

Eventually Grandpa showed up. And he cried too. But it wasn't a thing, because even though Grandpa isn't one for extra emotion when it's not necessary, that didn't apply here.

Because when you miss somebody and they come back from wherever they went, you don't have to pretend like it's not a big deal.

You can cry, damn it.

That's what Grandpa would have said, but he was too busy crying too.

SEVENTEEN

GRANDPA EVENTUALLY TOLD US to take a walk so we could talk, and even though there was so much to say, we didn't feel like we were in a rush to get back to normal right away.

We sat down on the curb outside school where I normally sit with Fil, and we just got used to being next to each other again.

"Do you know why I named you Walter?" he asked after a while.

"No," I said. It sounded strange hearing myself say that. It seemed like something I should have asked about or been curious about at some point.

He folded his hands and looked at me and said, "Your grandpa suggested it."

"What?"

It didn't seem like something Dad would listen to anyone else about.

"Well, he didn't exactly pick Walter, but he told me *how* to pick Walter. He said to choose a name that meant something. A song I liked. A musician I liked. A place. Something that makes me feel good when I think about it because, no matter what, somebody is going to say they don't like it."

"So, what makes you feel good about the name Walter?" I asked. I thought it might be some musician that nobody knew about whose name was Walter.

"There was this guy who lived in the bus stop near our apartment. He sang folk songs every morning."

I'm pretty sure my eyes rolled all the way to the back of my head, because this was weird even for him.

"Dad, you named me after a random guy from the bus stop?"

"No," he said. "I named you after his dog."

I opened my mouth, but before I could even form the word "what," Dad was already laughing. Big laughs. The kind that grow inside you and you have to let out slowly so you can breathe.

"Hear me out," Dad said, when he could talk

again. "I listened to the guy every day. And his music was good. It was a nice way to start the morning, but what I noticed was the way the dog really seemed to be into it when he played and how much he looked like he loved sitting with this guy. So I asked him about the dog, and he said, 'He's the reason I play. He's the reason I get up every morning.' And that was it. So I asked him the dog's name."

"Then I'm really lucky it was Walter and not Flutternutter."

Dad laughed again.

"You have always been the reason I play, Walter. You're the reason I get up every morning. And you're the reason I had to go away for a while, so that when I got back I could be better. For you."

I didn't say anything, because I didn't need to.

It's great being happy because you're finally back with someone you missed. It's probably better than Christmas or birthdays or surprises. It's one of those feelings that you want to hold on to forever.

Dad put his arm around me, and we sat outside the school for a few minutes before I looked around for Grandpa, who was leaning against the painted kindergarten wall behind us. He was smiling.

"Ready to go, Dad?" Dad said. Sometimes I forget Grandpa was a dad first.

Grandpa nodded, looking up at the stars, and then said, "Wish we could grab a donut."

"It's not even Sunday," I said.

"Doesn't have to be," said Grandpa.

Then we all piled in the truck and drove home.

But on Sunday, I was definitely going to get something with sprinkles. Or maybe the chocolate one with Bavarian cream.

EIGHTEEN

IT'S BEEN A WEEK since Dad had moved into Grandpa's house with us, and it isn't perfect, because he and Grandpa get on each other's nerves a lot. But I'm happy.

A few days after he moved in, when I had already gone to bed, I could hear Dad playing music downstairs. I thought Grandpa had already gone to bed too, but he was sitting in his armchair listening to Dad play with his eyes closed while Tiberius sat curled up in his lap.

I know that doesn't seem like much, but it is.

Fil thought so, too.

She said, "Men have a hard time processing emotions."

I told her she sounded like a nerd.

She told me that's a compliment.

Dad says being an alcoholic is like having a disease.

An alcoholic is someone who drinks too much.

He says it takes over everything until you make excuses for it, and it becomes so much a part of you that you can't avoid it even though you want to. Like trying to run away from your own skin, he said.

I can't picture that.

He says it's like being sick but not looking sick.

"You don't ever really get better," he said. "You just keep fighting back against that thing inside you that wants you to do the bad thing. That's why you get help. And why you have to keep getting help."

"And that's why you go to meetings?" I asked.

"Yep," he said.

He got an interview to host a morning radio show, and even though it's not music, he seemed excited about it. He turned down an offer to tour with another band on the East Coast because he didn't want to go anywhere without me again, and he thought Apple Grove was really good for me.

"You going to let Mrs. Butte help out with the announcements?" Dad asked.

I had filled him in on every tiny detail he'd missed

since he'd been gone, and one of them was that Mrs. Butte, the front desk lady, really seemed to hate my guts. But Dad listened to the story, and when I told him that she used to do the announcements whenever the Announcement Kid couldn't, he shook his head.

"She misses it," he said. "She likes filling in."

Grown-ups aren't that different from kids. I think they get jealous too. And they get used to stuff. And they get offended and mad and don't know how to respond to it when someone takes something away that they shouldn't care about. But they do. And that's what I realized when Dad said that. When I looked at the old log of morning announcements with a list of all the highlights, every single list said it was read by A. Butte.

Such a terrible name.

She was the one who did the majority of the morning announcements before I got to Apple Grove. She pretended not to care about that. She even pretended it was some kind of hassle, but she actually liked doing it. So there's only one thing you can do when you realize you hurt somebody even though you didn't mean to. You try to fix it even if you're the kid and they are the grown-up.

So starting now, she does the first part with the date and the weather, and I do the funny part.

I think Dad was right. I don't think she hates me anymore.

Good Morning, Apple Grove Performing Arts Academy!

This is Sam, your super squirrel mascot, reminding you to work hard in your physical education test today!

GO NUTS!

Also, today's specials are meat loaf, grilled cheese, and salads.

Thanks, Apple Grove.

Have an awesome day.

Seriously. Go for it.

I knew Fil was going to say my squirrel voice was good, and that Dad was going to ask me to do it for him later, and that Grandpa was going to take me climbing right after school because even though we both suck, it's a routine now and we have to keep going.

And I knew that the orange journal wasn't magic, but when I flipped to a page this morning, it said:

I love you, Walter.

Because Dad had written it there himself. Sometimes that's all that matters.

SOME ORANGE JOURNAL ENTRIES THAT DIDN'T MAKE IT INTO THE STORY BUT ARE WORTH NOTING:

Not everyone is going to care about what you care about. Try not to let that bother you.

At middle school dances, we all moved like zombies, facing each other with hands on our partner's shoulders, drifting side to side. I remember understanding that it was my task to choose a partner to dance with, and if she agreed to the arrangement, it was then our responsibility to avoid eye contact for an entire song.

I still sleep in the fetal position, because when I was little, I was afraid of the cartoon ballerina hippos in Fantasia. Let me explain. For some reason they freaked me out, and I convinced myself they were at the foot of my bed under my blanket, hence the fetal position. The size of the hippopotamus did not occur to me, nor did the implausibility of merely bending my legs saving me from a hippo attack. But it made perfect sense to six-year-old me.

If you ever become an elementary school teacher, don't blame the whole class for one dude being a turd.

Hummus is not overrated.

People have really strong opinions about pineapple on pizza.

I always forget that Rice Krispies treats are a thing. Then they show up again, and five seconds after I eat one, it immediately disappears from my memory. What are they? Sweet air bubbles?

I love clocks, and I'm a little sad we have no use for them anymore. There was a time when I was a kid when I wanted to own my own clock shop. Like with big grandfather clocks and the little cuckoo clocks that chime the hour with a weird little bird that pops out. Now we have phones, which are way better, but nothing ticks anymore. The ticking was kinda therapeutic.

It is NEVER the right time to tell me that the thing I am currently eating once gave you diarrhea.

ACKNOWLEDGMENTS

A giant, heartfelt thank you to the following people:

The fabulous and talented Harper Team! Especially David Linker, my editor, who saw the faint trace of magic in the messy drafts. It has been a privilege to work with you. Editorial assistants Carter Wilken and Sherry Fisher, who provided notes along the way. Heather Tamarkin and Mary Magrisso, the production editors, and Ana Deboo, the copyeditor who made sure everything lined up. Copyeditors are heroes. (All the leftover mistakes are my own.) Corina Lupp, Alison Klapthor, Emily Mannon, and Jenny Lu for all their hard work on Design, Marketing, and Publicity. Thank you for blessing me with your artistic talents and your tireless efforts to get Walter into the hands of as many readers as possible. And, of course, Lesley Vamos, the glorious artist who created the cover of my dreams. Could not have imagined a more perfect image of Walter. It blew me away. This book would not be on a shelf without you all.

Jodi Reamer, my super-agent, who patiently responds to panicked emails and acts as my whimsical guide on this crazy writing journey.

My teachers, every single teacher I have ever had. Even if you tried to teach me math. THANK YOU.

My librarians (AND ALL LIBRARIANS), especially Ms. O, who is no doubt recommending Judy Blume in heaven right now.

Musical Theater. This is a catch-all for the musicals I love and all the musicals I have yet to love. Every actor, director, writer, musician responsible for keeping theater and Broadway alive.

The Orange County School of Performing Arts. I miss you. I hope to be back someday. Your students and staff are outrageously talented.

Orange County Children's Theater, for being an amazing foundation for theater kids.

Kerbanu Pudumjee, for the use of her fabulous name.

Nick Naveda, for reading one of the very first drafts and being encouraging as always.

Lauren Moffat, for reading the almost final draft,

catching typos, and boosting my confidence.

My grown-ups: Linda and Mike, who nurtured my creativity by giving me a lifelong love of books and the freedom to make messes. Thanks for all the bedtime stories. They're in my heart forever.

Margaret and Doug, for their unconditional love and support throughout my entire adult life. Mahalo for sharing Hawaii with me and for being there when we need you.

My grandparents, Adelia and Pete, for all the childhood memories at your house in the summer. My Boulia, the best storyteller of all time.

My sisters, Athena and Cassandra, the guardians of my ego. Always keeping it in check. Always. I love you . . . and Ouch.

My kids, Alex, Charlie, and Jamie. You make writing almost impossible and everything else unforgettable. I love you.

Olina, an absolute angel on earth.

My husband Doug, a logical Spock-like creature who keeps our lives running with unparalleled efficiency. Thanks for driving so I can look out the window.